upsetting annie

Other books in the growing Faithgirlz!™ library

Best Friends Bible
The Faithgirlz!™ Bible
NIV Faithgirlz!™ Backpack Bible
My Faithgirlz!™ Journal

The Blog On Series

Grace Notes (Book One)
Love, Annie (Book Two)
Just Jazz (Book Three)
Storm Rising (Book Four)
Grace Under Pressure (Book Five)

Nonfiction

No Boy's Allowed: Devotions for Girls
Girlz Rock: Devotions for You
Chick Chat: More Devotions for Girls
Shine On, Girl!: Devotions to Keep You Sparkling

Check out www.faithgirlz.com

faiThGirLz!

upsetting annie

DANDI DALEY MACKALL

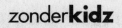

zonderkidz

ZONDERVAN.com/
AUTHORTRACKER
follow your favorite authors

The children's group of Zondervan

www.zonderkidz.com

Upsetting Anie
Copyright © 2007 by Dandi Daley Mackall
Illustrations © 2007 by Zondervan

Requests for information should be addressed to:
Zonderkidz
Grand Rapids, Michigan 49530

Library of Congress Cataloging-in-Publication Data

Mackall, Dandi Daley.
Upsetting Annie / by Dandi Daley Mackall.
    p. cm. -- (Blog on series ; bk. 6) (Faithgirlz!)
    Summary: Everything seems to be going well for fifteen-year-old Annie, between her popular blog, good friends, and cheerleading, but when her cousin Shawna returns from Paris and becomes the center of attention, Annie cannot help but be jealous.
    ISBN-13: 978-0-310-71264-0 (softcover)
    ISBN-10: 0-310-71264-5 (softcover)
    [1. Blogs--Fiction. 2. Popularity--Fiction. 3. Jealousy--Fiction. 4. Cousins--Fiction. 5. High schools--Fiction. 6. Schools--Fiction. 7. Christian life--Fiction. 8. Ohio--Fiction]   I. Title.
    PZ7.M1905Ups 2007
    [Fic]--dc22

                                                                                    2006020339

Editor: Barbara Scott
Art direction: Laura Maitner-Mason
Illustrator: Julie Speer
Cover design: Karen Phillips
Interior design: Pamela J.L. Eicher

Illustrations used in this book were created in Adobe Illustrator.
The body text for this book is set in Cochin Medium.

Printed in the United States of America

07 08 09 10 11 • 5 4 3 2 1

So we fix our eyes not on what is seen, but on what is unseen. For what is seen is temporary, but what is unseen is eternal.

— 2 Corinthians 4:18

1

Dear Professor Love,

Life is SO not fair! My 2 sisters have boyfriends. They've always had boyfriends. And when they break up (They always do the breaking. Nobody ever breaks up with them!), they get new boyfriends within the week. They have dates every weekend. The only dates I have are pity dates, when my friends fix me up with their guy friends. I've suffered through so many blind dates, my sisters say I should get a guide dog.

What should I do?

—Boyfriendless

Dear Boyfriendless,

Take a deep breath, girlfriend! I know where you're coming from because I've been there. But I'm working

*on changing my tune. Why do we think we have 2 have
boyfriends? Sounds like your sisters aren't doing so well
in that department if they're breaking up all the time,
right? Maybe you and those friends of yours should stop
the blind date train and just go out together. Have fun!
Develop friendships with guys. BTW, a date can be the
worst place for friendships! And breakups can be the
worst thing for friends.*

*But maybe your sisters are right about 1 thing. Get a
dog — dogs rock!*

Love, Professor Love

Annie Lind leaned back and admired her work as Professor
Love. The whole *That's What You Think!* blog team had met
at the cottage earlier, like they did most Saturday mornings.
Annie had taken up half the time telling them her big news: her
cousin Shawna would be coming to Big Lake for the summer.
Annie didn't know if she could wait two whole months.

Since she still had an hour to kill before cheerleading
practice, Annie hung around after the meeting was over. She
adored the cottage, with its giant fireplace, wooden beams,
and white stucco walls. It belonged to Gracie's bio mom, who
was off in Europe someplace. The cottage was perfect for
writing her love advice column.

She got back to it.

Dear Professor Love,

*I'm in love with Jennifer. And I totally trust her. It's just
that there are so many guys at my school who would*

*like to have my Jennifer. And she's so friendly with
everybody. I get crazy when I see her talking with some
guy by her locker or in the cafeteria or after school. When
I can't find Jen, or I call her and she doesn't pick up, or
I drive by her house and see her car gone, I fly into a
jealous rage. I'm afraid my jealousy will drive her away.*

*Is it expecting too much for her to let me know where she
is at all times?*

— Watchdog

Annie didn't even have to think about this one. She set her
fingers to the keyboard.

Dear Watchdog,

*Hmm . . . Is it 2 much 2 expect for you 2 know where
Jennifer is at all times? Of course not — as long as she's in
prison. That's the only way you can be sure where she is
every minute.*

*Sounds like the problem isn't Jennifer. It's you, Watchdog!
You're jealous without cause. I suggest you get a grip.
Actually, I suggest you loosen that grip!*

Love, Professor Love

Dear Professor Love,

*Why is life so unfair? I'm a nice person. I'm not hot, but
i'm okay to look at. Still, my whole life it's seemed like
everybody is more popular than i am. When girls hit the*

mall, nobody thinks 2 ask me. I'm left out when they go 2 a game together or just hang out before school. I wish i could trade lives. It's always been like this. If there are three of us, i'm the odd girl out. Hey — when i was little, i had two imaginary friends. They wouldn't let me play with them.

— The unfair maiden

Annie laughed out loud at that one. Then she typed her answer:

Dear Maiden,

Don't trade places with anyone! Sounds to me as if you have a great sense of humor. (I LOL at your exclusive imaginary friends!)

Most people in middle school and high school feel like the odd person out. (It's one of the best kept secrets of high school!) Don't forget that you're exactly the person God wants you to be. You think God makes mistakes? No way! Without you, there would be a hole in the universe!

Love, Professor Love

Annie stopped typing and glanced through the rest of the e-mails in her "Professor Love" pile. There was a question — more like a gripe — from a kid who studied hard for B's, while his brother got A's without studying. Somebody who called herself Two-Ton began her e-mail with the same two words that kept popping up: *No fair!*

"Gracie!" Annie shouted. She *had* to see this. Annie scrolled down and found another e-mail complaining about life's unfairness. "Gracie! I think I've got our blog theme!"

That did it. Annie heard the squeak of chair legs on the wood floor, followed by Gracie's footsteps overhead.

"You better not be playing me, Prof," Gracie warned, bounding down the stairs two at a time. In seconds, she was reading over Annie's shoulder. "I'd just about given up on a theme."

When they'd ended the blog meeting, Gracie's instructions had been for everybody to write their columns, and she'd figure out a theme later. Several months ago Grace Doe had started the anonymous blog with the help of her little sister, Mick, the computer guru. Annie, Storm, and Jazz had been brought on board later. Gracie, the unofficial boss, could be officially bossy, especially about blog themes. But this time Annie felt sure she had the perfect theme.

"No fair!" Annie said. Gracie narrowed her green eyes at Annie. Annie thought Gracie's eyes were her best feature. That, and her relatively small feet. But then Annie noticed everybody's feet because they were all smaller than her own.

"You called me down here to complain?" Gracie inhaled, as if not choking her friend required superpowers. "I was in the middle of my blog, Annie! What's so unfair?"

"I'm not complaining. That's the theme — *No fair*!" Annie pointed to the screen, where her "Professor Love" column was still displayed. Gracie moved in closer. She shoved her short, straight blonde hair off her forehead and frowned as she read.

"Hmmm. Might work. I'm liking it." She moved the curser. "Cool. No fair. Should be easy to blog on that." Finally, she grinned at Annie. "Not bad."

"Aw, you don't have to gush, Gracie," Annie teased. Gracie's dimple showed, even though Annie could tell how hard she was trying to maintain her tough-guy blog editor persona.

The door flew open, and Gracie's little stepsis, Mick, rushed in. Sweat glistened on her forehead, even though all she wore were jeans and her Cleveland Indians T-shirt.

"Mick, where's your jacket?" Gracie called.

"Outside. With Ty. We're getting in some great batting practice. I just came back to get us something to drink. You should see Ty's swing! He's going to hit hard this spring." Mick kicked off her shoes and dashed through to the kitchen.

Annie knew Mick would have played ball all day and night if she could have. Mick felt about baseball the way Annie did about cheerleading. "Hey, Mick! Is it nice out?" March in Big Lake, Ohio, could bring spring in the morning and snow at noon.

"Annie?" Mick squinted into the room. She wasn't wearing her glasses. Probably because she'd broken three pairs so far this year playing ball. "I didn't even see you there. Sorry! Why aren't you at cheerleading practice?"

"It doesn't start 'til ten."

Mick frowned. "Are you sure? Ty and I were playing catch behind the gym. It sure sounded like cheerleading practice."

Annie glanced at the clock. 9:40. "That doesn't make any sense. Bridget told me last night that practice wouldn't start until — "

"Bridget?" Grace interrupted. "As in Bridget Crawford?"

Annie nodded.

Gracie sighed. "Annie, how many times do I have to tell you, listen to that girl's body language, not her words? Didn't you tell me she's angling for your spot on the squad? The pyramid topper, or whatever you call it?"

"Flyer." Annie had been a flyer since the fall. By rights, the position shouldn't have gone to a sophomore. Or to anyone as tall as Annie. But she was fearless, lightweight, and peppy.

Ms. Whitney, their coach, said nobody smiled more than Annie on the court. Nobody had more expressions, which was a big part of flying during stunts. Still, Annie knew she'd have to fight to keep her position.

"I can't believe I let Bridget pull this on me!" She fumbled with her bag, stuffing everything back in. *"Annie's Rule: Never believe a rival!* Why don't I listen to myself?" She slipped one arm into her jacket.

Mick opened the door for her. "Maybe Bridget got the times mixed up."

"Right." Annie could have kicked herself for falling for it. This was vintage Bridget. "Later, guys! This is war!"

Annie raced to Big Lake High. The sun peeked in and out of moving clouds that covered most of the sky. The trees weren't fooled by the sunshine. The only leaves were brown hangers-on from fall.

Outside the gymnasium, Annie paused just long enough to catch her breath. Inside, the squeak of tennis shoes echoed off the walls, and Ms. Whitney's voice barked out orders: "Arms straight! Chin up! Eyes on the flyer!"

Eyes on the flyer?

But they didn't have the flyer. *Annie* was the flyer. Annie shoved open the gym door just in time to see the Big Lake Sharks cheerleaders finishing their new tumbling routine. And right in the center — just like they'd been practicing for competition — stood the mini-pyramid, Elevator. With Bridget on top.

"There's Annie!" Rakiah shouted from her position as back spotter.

"Focus, people!" Ms. Whitney commanded.

"Let me go up again! I want to try a heel stretch, Ms. Whitney!" Bridget shouted. She was doing a simple Liberty: one knee bent, arms raised like the Statue of Liberty. It was the stunt Annie always pulled for the finale of their competition routine.

Annie couldn't do heel stretches. Ms. Whitney had been fine with the Liberty.

"I don't think we'll go there, Bridget," Ms. Whitney answered. "Ready for the dismount?"

The spotter and bases closed in, and Bridget dropped to the blue mat in the center of the gym floor. She landed on her feet — her *tiny* feet — and spun into a cartwheel and round-off.

Annie glared at her.

"You're late, Annie," Ms. Whitney said, straightening the mats she always spread before practice. She was petite, five foot three, but she made up for it with a booming voice. This was her first year teaching, and she could have passed for an Ohio State cheerleader, which she'd been for three years. "Well, don't just stand there!"

Annie glanced over at Bridget, who was biting her lip. Her blonde ponytail swished as her eyes darted from Ms. Whitney to Annie.

Annie thought about ratting Bridget out, telling Ms. Whitney that Bridget had given her the wrong practice time on purpose. Instead, she waved. "Hey, Bridget!" Annie enjoyed the totally baffled look on Bridget's face. Better to let the girl sweat it out and wonder. *Annie's Rule.* "Thanks for covering for me. Sorry I'm late, everybody. Won't happen again. I guarantee that." She smiled meaningfully in Bridget's direction.

"Good. Because in case you forgot, we have our first competition one week from today." Ms. Whitney grabbed her right heel with her left hand and pulled up and across her body in a perfect Bow and Arrow.

Annie wished she were half that limber, or a tenth that graceful. She did stretching exercises morning and night, but she just wasn't limber enough. Rakiah told Annie she made a good flyer because she stayed stiff for the lifts. Annie knew she put in more hours than any of the other girls. But there were some things she'd never be able to pull off.

Ms. Whitney clapped her hands. "I know this is your first competition. I don't expect us to take first place, although I wouldn't complain if we did. But I do expect a strong showing. The other Ohio schools will have lots of tumbling in their routines. So let's get to work on ours!"

Rakiah jogged over to help Annie roll out the long, blue padded mat. "How come you were late?" Rakiah asked.

"Bridget," Annie answered.

Rakiah's eyes doubled in size. "What did she do?"

"Doesn't matter," Annie mumbled. "She won't do it again."

Rakiah was five foot five and a terrific gymnast. Her feet were at least three sizes smaller than Annie's. Something about her reminded Annie of her cousin, maybe because Annie had talked about Shawna all morning.

"Rakiah," she said, smoothing a wrinkle in the old mat, "did I ever tell you that you remind me of my cousin Shawna?"

"I didn't know you had a cousin, Annie. Where's she live?"

"She's in Paris now, but she lives in New Orleans."

"Does she ever get to Big Lake?"

Annie grinned. "As a matter of fact, she's going to spend the whole summer with me."

They tumbled the length of the mats, one after the other. Then they formed their lines for the routines they'd rehearsed backward and forward. Annie felt confident with the dance routines. She'd practiced enough so her big feet didn't get in the way. Nobody on the squad worked harder than she did to get the cheers and routines down. But Annie knew that nobody *needed* to work harder. Little baseball-playing Mick had more athletic ability in her big toe than Annie had in her entire body. She finished right on cue, making sure she shouted the cheers louder than anybody:

> *"We're from Big Lake! Sharks are us!*
> *Listen while we make a fuss!*
> *Big Lake! Big Lake! Shake your fin!*
> *Come on, Sharks, and win, win, win!"*

Annie had written that cheer after cheerleading camp, picking up on a chant they'd learned there.

"Are we done yet?" asked Amanda, one of the senior cheerleaders. She did the best back handsprings, so she got to go last in the tumble lines during their three-minute competition routine. They didn't have anybody who could do a standing tuck, landing on their feet with no hands. But Amanda could pull half a dozen back handsprings in a row without going out of line.

A couple of the girls chimed in with Amanda, claiming they'd practiced long enough. Not Annie. She never wanted to quit. She loved being a cheerleader, and she loved everything about cheering, even practice.

Even tryouts. When she'd gone out for the varsity squad last year as a freshman, twenty-two girls had tried out for the two open spots on the squad. Annie had been scared to death. She couldn't do a back handspring or true splits. But she'd made the squad anyway, with a bouncy attitude and loads of spirit.

This year at tryouts she tripped, and the student body still elected her sophomore cheerleader. Annie wasn't kidding herself. She made cheerleader because kids liked her, not because she was so great at it. But what she lacked in natural ability, she made up for in hard work and enthusiasm. At least she hoped so.

When the other girls had voted for Annie to be flyer, she'd been so grateful that she'd prayed right there on the gym floor. Since then, she'd had time to think about it. She figured at least part of the reason they'd made her flyer was that she wasn't strong enough to be a good base.

Ms. Whitney had the girls rearrange the mats. "Don't forget! We have a game Tuesday. We can't let the guys down just because we have to work on our competition stunts."

"You said it, Coach!"

Annie looked toward the obviously male voice coming from the hallway and saw half a dozen guys standing in the doorway, watching. They all played Big Lake Sharks varsity basketball.

"Tell me something. How much practice does it take to say 'Rah!' and jump around?" This comment came from Greg,

a sophomore who had dated Bridget at the beginning of the
year. Annie decided it was too bad they'd broken up. They
were obviously made for each other.

"Why don't you come out here, and we'll show you what a
real sport's like?" Annie called back.

Most of the cheerleaders seconded that: "That's right!"
"You tell him, Annie!"

"We really don't practice that much, Greg," Annie
continued. "Only on days that end in a *y*."

Liam, a tall junior Annie had a smile-in-the-hallway
relationship with, bowed to the cheerleaders. "Pardon us,
Miss Annie." He'd moved to Ohio from Kentucky, bringing
his adorable southern accent with him. "Greg here does not
speak for the rest of us. We deeply appreciate y'all's skill
and dedication, without which basketball would not be
basketball."

Annie returned the bow. She'd been trying to keep herself
boyfriend free for over a month. It had paid off too. She'd
developed friendships with a couple of guys in her church,
and she'd gotten to know some BLHS guys better too. But
Liam Wilson was making it harder and harder to keep to the
friendship track.

Ms. Whitney banished the guys to the locker room and
ran the cheerleaders through their new welcome cheer for
Tuesday's game. They finished off with a low version of the
Totem Pole that placed Annie in a knee stand on Bridget's
and Callie's backs.

"Ouch!" Bridget cried, just as the cheer ended.

Ms. Whiney moved in closer. "What's wrong?"

"It's Annie," Bridget whined.

Rakiah rushed to Annie's defense. "Annie's light as a feather, Bridget, and you know it."

"I didn't say she wasn't light," Bridget grumbled. "It's her big foot. It always ends up where it shouldn't."

Annie's cheeks felt on fire.

"Well, it looked good," Ms. Whitney said. "Annie, maybe you could try setting your knee a little higher on Bridget? Should we call it a day?"

"No!" Annie said it louder than she'd meant to. "I mean, if we're really going to do the Liberty at halftime, shouldn't we do it one more time?" Most high schools had banned stunting, except in competition. Ms. Whitney had only let them pull the Liberty one other time, and that was for homecoming. She was only letting them do it in tomorrow's game as a kind of practice for competition.

Amanda and Bridget groaned, but the others were up for it.

Annie, as top girl, walked into her bases, Callie and Bridget, for the lift. Callie made a great base, and Annie trusted her totally. And no matter how Annie felt about Bridget, the girl was a strong base. Rakiah stayed close behind as a spotter, ready to catch the flyer if anything went wrong. Annie could hardly wait for that moment when she felt like she was flying.

On exactly the right count, Callie and Bridget dipped, and Annie stepped into their hands. She kept her body stiff as she was lifted on one leg, straight up, her other leg tucked beneath her, arms extended in the Liberty. She felt the breeze as she flew head and shoulders above everybody. There was no feeling on earth like this. She even felt closer to God, as if she and God were alone in space.

"Watch your big feet!" Bridget snapped from below.

Annie's thoughts jerked back to earth. To her feet. In her mind, she saw Bridget doing the Liberty. Bridget with her small feet. And just that fast, she no longer felt herself flying. She was the big-footed oaf trying to stand on too-small bases.

"Annie?" Rakiah's voice sounded far away.

Someone else was saying Annie's name too. Callie maybe? Or Bridget?

As if she were in a thick fog, standing in a lake of Jell-O, Annie's knees wobbled under her. She watched her hands thrashing the air, but they seemed to belong to someone else.

The last thing Annie saw was the blue of the mat rushing up at her, pulling her into it at the speed of dark.

"Are you okay?" Rakiah apologized to Annie over and over. "It's the spotter's job — *my* job — to make sure you don't fall! What happened?"

Annie brushed herself off and got to her feet. "Not to worry, Rakiah. I'm fine." She shook out her legs and shoulders. Nothing hurt. She'd caught herself on her feet and hands before crashing. She'd fallen like this a dozen times. More. Still, her hands were shaking.

"That was so knicked out!" Callie sounded like she was afraid someone would blame her. "Annie just went limp on us."

Ms. Whitney hovered over Annie. "You sure you're okay? You look a little pale."

"I'm fine." The words came out a whisper. She cleared her throat and tried again. "I'm okay." Of course, she was okay. Flyers fell all the time.

"I should have caught you," Rakiah said.

Annie made herself smile up at Rakiah, whose black hair framed her dark face. "Not your fault. I lost it." She tried to remember those seconds before the fall — the breeze against her cheek, the sensation of flying. She remembered wondering how her Liberty compared with Bridget's. Then everything fell apart.

"Spotters, you know that no matter how this happened, it's your job to catch the flyer, right? And bases, where were you?" Ms. Whitney frowned at Bridget.

Bridget had been hanging back. "Annie, I'm sorry. Did I move? I didn't mean to. Your toe brushed the side of my head on the lift, and I said something to you. But I didn't think I moved."

Now Annie remembered the comment about her "big feet." It would have been great to blame the fall on Bridget. But she couldn't. Annie shook her head. "You didn't do anything." Annie just wanted to make it blow over. "Will you guys stop making a big deal of this? Cheering's a contact sport, right? People fall." She forced a big smile and saw the chain reaction of relieved smiles around her. "So, when's our next practice?"

Ms. Whitney handed out schedules for the week. "I don't want anybody showing up late. We need every minute of every practice if we don't want to embarrass ourselves at competition."

They broke off in twos and threes. Sasha and Rakiah walked out with Annie.

"Want to stay and watch the guys practice?" Sasha asked.

"I'd rather hit the mall," Rakiah said. "Annie, do you have the car?"

Annie shook her head. "Nope. Mom's got it at the shop." Samantha Lind owned and operated Sam's Sammich Shop, the number-one hangout for Big Lake students.

"We could go to Sam's," Sasha suggested. "I could use some ice cream."

"I promised Storm I'd meet her after her shift at Big Lake Foods," Annie said. "We could meet you there later."

Sasha and Rakiah headed toward the shop, and Annie walked the opposite direction, west toward Big Lake's only supermarket. She was glad for the chance to be alone. She needed to think. She'd fallen — big deal! — she'd fallen dozens of times in practice. She had the bruises to prove it.

So what was it about this fall that made her so ... so ... so what?

So puzzled?

So confused?

So rattled?

So shook up?

She needed to pray. Annie stopped in the parking lot of the supermarket and closed her eyes. Immediately, she pictured the blue mat rushing up at her. Her head swirled.

Honk!

She opened her eyes and jogged to the sidewalk.

Michael, an ex-boyfriend, stuck his head out the window of a white pickup. "Hey, Annie! No sleeping in the parking lot!" he shouted.

Annie managed a fake laugh and a halfhearted wave. She had to get a grip.

With her eyes open this time, Annie prayed: *Father, thanks for letting me land on the mat and not get hurt. The deal is, I'm kind of rattled. I didn't see that fall coming, and I can't get it out of my head. So I need —*

"Lost?"

Annie looked up in time to see Grace Doe, dressed as usual in a camouflage jacket and black jeans. "Hey, Gracie. You working today?"

Gracie glanced at her watch. "In five minutes."

They walked in together. Annie could feel Gracie's gaze on her. Grace Doe was an observer. She didn't talk much, but she didn't miss a thing.

"Trouble?" Gracie asked.

"Not really. Just not my best day at cheerleading practice."

Gracie glanced sideways at her. "There's more to this story."

Annie shrugged. It was eerie the way Gracie could read people. "I fell, Gracie. That's all."

"Ah."

"What do you mean, 'Ah'?" Annie demanded.

Gracie raised her eyebrows and kept walking through the glass doors that swooshed open automatically. Annie trailed behind her. She dodged a row of shopping carts being pushed into the cart corral.

"Go ahead," Annie said. "Tell me how stupid it is to hurt myself in the futile pursuit of cheerleading." She and Gracie had had this conversation more than once. Gracie was such a loner. It was a miracle they'd become friends.

"Stupid?" Gracie held her hand over her heart in mock amazement. "Why would I think it's stupid to jump up and down and scream poor rhymes in public? Especially when said activity leaves one black and blue? Lots of people like black and blue."

"Tell me again why I'm talking to you." Annie elbowed her friend. In spite of herself, Gracie had made her feel better.

"Must be my charm," Gracie answered. She slid behind the customer service stall, shed her jacket, and grabbed the green service shirt. "Gotta go. As always, a pleasure to converse with you, Ms. Lind."

Gracie took up her spot as bagger next to the woman with huge, beehive hair. Annie didn't follow her. Gracie was all business once she started her shift.

Not so with Storm Novelo. Even if Annie hadn't known where to look for Storm — in the checkout aisle behind Gracie's — she would have figured it out as soon as she spotted the long line. Storm's checkout always had the most people in line. She was the most popular bagger in Big Lake, and not only with the guys. Regulars came through just to be entertained by Storm, who didn't disappoint. She had a story or trivia fact for every food item that came through.

As usual, Storm, who was mestiza — part Spanish and part Mayan — looked exotic, with her shiny, purple-streaked black hair hanging to her waist. Even her lime green stretch pants and canary peasant blouse worked for her, although Annie couldn't imagine the outfit on anybody else.

"Annie! What's happening?" Storm shouted.

"Go on," the customer urged. "How long *would* it reach if they lined up each stick of gum sold last year?" The man looked older than Gramps Lind by at least a decade.

Storm dropped a pack of Wrigley's into a small brown bag. "That gum line would reach around the world nineteen times!" she answered dramatically.

"Is that right?" He shook his head and took the bag from Storm. Annie wondered if he made such a small purchase so he could come back more often.

Annie scooted onto the ledge under the store window, where she could be close enough to hear the "Storm Novelo Show."

The next person in line was a boy Annie guessed to be
about twelve. She wondered if he belonged to the old man
who'd just left because all the kid had was a pack of bubble
gum. "Bet you don't know why bubble gum is pink," he said.

"You again?" Storm laughed. "Sorry. I know this one too,
Ben. Pink was the only color the inventor had left after trying
to come up with his own stretchy version of gum. He was
stuck with it. Get it? Stuck?"

"Lucky guess," Ben said. "But you won't know this one.
Who was presented with the biggest piece of gum in the
world?"

Storm crossed her eyes at him. "Willie Mays, 1974, the size
of 10,000 normal pieces of gum."

"How do you know this stuff?" The kid sounded frustrated.

Annie used to wonder the same thing. Trivia seemed to leak
out of Storm's brain. Her part of the *That's What You Think!*
website was to write trivia columns. She hardly ever had to
look up anything. But Annie had finally seen through Storm's
ditzy act and realized the girl read. And read. Storm checked
out reference books from the library and read everything she
got her hands on, including the ketchup bottles at the shop.

The boy snatched his gum before Storm could bag it. He
tore into the pack, unwrapped a piece, stuck it in his mouth,
and chewed hard.

Storm reached over the counter and scruffed the kid's hair.
"You better get yourself some of that new Japanese gum,
Ben. Mood gum. We don't have it yet. But it changes colors
when you change moods."

"Cool!"

"Move along, please," said the cashier.

"Okay. Okay," Ben said, shuffling a few feet to the end of the counter. "Just tell me another word for gum. One you haven't given me already."

Storm scratched her head. *"Heung how chu.* That's Chinese. Or *tuggumi,* in Swedish."

The kid went away smiling, chewing, and repeating the Chinese and Swedish words for gum. Just your normal day at the supermarket.

The next guy wore a Big Lake University letter jacket and was way too cute to be grocery shopping alone. He grinned at Storm like he knew her. "I don't want any chewing gum trivia, Storm," he said, his voice deep and dreamy. "I've had a lousy week. I need a joke."

Storm didn't even stop to think. "Okay. Why did the chewing gum cross the road?"

"This better be good," the guy said, showing two dimples.

"Because it was stuck to the chicken's leg!" Storm finished.

The guy was still laughing when he walked out of the store.

Annie was grateful for Storm's chatter. For five whole minutes she hadn't thought about her fall. But just that fast, the thought squeezed its way back inside her brain. And with it came a panic that made her feel like she was falling all over again.

4

"Five, four, three, two, one!" Storm shouted.

The people in her line groaned. Half of them peeled off to other lines.

"I am *so* out of here!" Storm announced. The cashier said something to her, and Storm unpinned her name tag and tossed it into the drawer. "Bye, Gracie!" she hollered, about ten times as loud as necessary.

Gracie didn't stop bagging, but called back, "See you, Storm. Get your article done!"

Storm grabbed her furry jacket from under the counter then dashed over to Annie. "Wouldn't Gracie make an out-of-sight general?"

Annie hopped off the window ledge. "She's all that." Annie felt self-conscious walking next to Storm, who was barely five foot three. Storm Novelo would have made a great flyer, but she had no interest in cheerleading and had told Annie at least a dozen times that she wouldn't be caught dead in a Sharks cheerleading outfit.

"Gum?" Storm stuck a pack of purple gum in Annie's face as they stepped out into the March wind.

Annie stared at the gum, a memory fluttering at the corner of her brain, deciding if it would breeze in or float on by.

"I paid for it, if that's what you're worried about."

"Don't be knicked!" Annie said. Storm had changed so
much in the last couple of months. Not that she was so bad
before. Annie had liked her from the first day she'd blown
into school. That's what it had felt like too. Like a real storm
had come to Big Lake. Annie loved it that Storm had found
her way to Christ without losing any of her quirkiness. She
was even more "Storm" than she had been before.

Storm kept holding out the gum. "What? You don't like
grape?"

Annie took a piece. "I do. Thanks." She folded the stick and
stuck it into her mouth. The thick grape smell took her back.
"I just remembered something. Shawna loves grape gum, or
she used to anyway."

"Shawna again? You can't stop thinking about that cousin,
can you?"

Annie knew she hadn't stopped talking about Shawna since
her mom had told her the big news a month earlier. Maybe
she'd been talking about her too much. She didn't want to
turn off her friends before they even met Shawna. "Sorry."

"I'm kidding," Storm said. "Tell me more about her."

Annie sighed. "I wish I knew more about her." She was
remembering the one time she and her mom had driven all the
way to New Orleans for Aunt Anne's wedding. Annie's dad
had died in a plane crash when Annie was two months old.
Uncle Jim, her dad's brother, died fourteen months later from
stomach cancer. When Aunt Anne married again, Shawna
and Annie must have been about five. The only thing Annie
remembered about the wedding was getting purple gum
stuck in her hair at the reception. Since then, she'd only seen
Shawna once, although the two families tried to stay in touch.

"Grape gum is one of the few things I know about my cousin," Annie admitted.

"Are you sure you're going to like having a stranger stay the whole summer with you?" Storm jogged ahead, then walked backward so she could face Annie. "What if she drives you postal? Or, like, she's taken up axe murdering as a hobby?"

Annie laughed. "She's no stranger, Storm! It will be like having a sister. I've always wanted a sister. I wrote Shawna twice in Paris and asked for her e-mail, but so far she hasn't written back. Letters take a long time to get to France. I told you that's where they've been since they left New Orleans, right?"

Storm nodded. They fell into step together. "Was Shawna in New Orleans when Hurricane Katrina hit?"

"Mom said they were caught trying to get out of the city. I guess they stayed in a football stadium, then motels for weeks."

They cut through the university, taking a shortcut to the shop. A couple of guys waved at Storm. She lifted her chin in a chin wave. "How did Shawna end up in Paris?"

Annie had told the whole blog team this, but Storm didn't always tune in. Not that Annie minded saying it again. "Shawna's school in New Orleans closed after the hurricane. Her stepdad's a pastor, but their church was pretty much destroyed. Most of their congregation moved away, so Shawna's parents decided it would be a good time to take this short-term mission gig in France and take Shawna with them."

"To Paris? That's so fly! I always think of missionaries heading off to Africa. If you can end up in Paris, I might have to seriously consider becoming a missionary."

They walked into the warmth of Sam's Sammich Shop, and Annie recognized the Beatles tune playing on the jukebox. Thanks to her mom's dedication to keeping the shop a flashback to the sixties, Annie knew every word to every Beatles and Beach Boys song ever written. She was shedding her jacket and humming along, when she realized something wasn't quite right. It was Saturday, the busiest day at the shop, but most of the tables were empty. "Where is every — ?"

Annie didn't finish her question because she saw the answer for herself. A small crowd was clustered around the ice-cream counter. People stood two and three deep by the counter stools. "What's going on?" she asked Storm.

"Let's find out!" Storm disappeared into the crowd.

Annie started to follow, but stopped when she heard her mom's voice: "I still can't believe it's really you!"

Annie couldn't imagine who Mom would be making such a fuss over. She tried to work her way through the crowd.

"Wait your turn," barked a woman with a nose so sharp it could have opened letters. The woman turned back to the counter and reached for something. Annie watched as she came away with a giant ice-cream cone ... without paying. The woman wasn't the only one getting ice cream. Most of the people in the crowd had cones or dishes.

A guy bumped Annie from behind. "Is this where they're giving out free ice cream?"

Free ice cream? Was Annie's mother — her watch-every-penny mother — giving away free ice cream? No way.

"Annie?" Mick the Munch waved from behind the ice-cream counter, then went back to scooping. Arms reached toward her like angry octopuses.

Annie tried to peer around a tall guy in a Middleview varsity jacket. He wouldn't budge. He was staring down at the end stool, or at someone on the stool. Annie couldn't tell which.

The crowd thinned as people grabbed their ice cream and wandered back to tables. She could hear them muttering:

"Thanks!"

"Hey, welcome to Big Lake!"

"Glad you're here! You'll love Ohio!"

The Middleview guy shouted over with a mouthful of ice cream, "I'll call you!"

Then Annie caught her first glimpse of the center of attention. From the back, all she could see was the girl's gorgeous, wavy brunette hair. She couldn't have been much taller than Mick, and her features were tiny. She was obviously cute, maybe even beautiful. But that didn't explain the fuss — or the free ice cream.

Feeling self-conscious, Annie made her way up to Mick. Storm had already gotten herself an ice-cream cone and managed to take over the stool next to the girl. "Is this spun, or what?" Storm asked. "Annie, have you been holding out on us, girl? Did you know she'd be here?"

Annie glanced from Storm to Mick to her mom. Finally, she let her gaze rest on the stranger. The girl on the end stool swiveled to face her. Her big green eyes turned to Annie, and suddenly Annie could picture her beautiful hair tangled in wads of purple gum.

"Shawna? What are you doing here?"

5

"Real nice, Annie," Storm teased. " 'What are you doing here?' That's how you greet your cousin?"

Annie ran over and hugged her cousin. "It's really you! Shawna! You got gorgeous on me!"

"I'll second that." Liam the Kentuckian hovered nearby.

"That's Liam," Annie confided. "He's a smooth talker. Better watch out for him."

"At least I won't be the only one with a southern drawl," Shawna said. Her accent was deeper South than Liam's. Annie thought it sounded musical.

Storm scooted over so Annie could sit by Shawna. Annie looked around for her mom. "Why didn't you tell me Shawna was here?"

Mom's eyes looked like one more tear would make them spill over. "I just found out myself last night. I don't think I could have kept it a secret another hour, though. Granny and Gramps wanted to surprise you."

"I'm surprised!" Her head felt light. "But I thought . . . I mean, weren't you supposed to . . . ?" A thousand questions pressed against her skull. *Why now? What happened to the summer plan? Where were her parents? Was she here to stay? What about school?* Annie didn't want to ask any of her questions because she didn't want her cousin to think — even for a second — that she wasn't wanted.

A crowd had built up again, and both Mick and Annie's mom were scooping ice cream now.

"Is that the new girl?" Sasha asked, reaching for her cone.

"It's Annie's cousin," Rakiah explained.

"New Girl." Storm repeated. "I like it. I was the last New Girl around here, and I'm cool with handing over the title."

Annie introduced Shawna to Sasha and Rakiah and a couple of the others pressed around the ice-cream counter.

Shawna smiled at each one. "Everybody's making me feel so welcome. Thanks, y'all. Aunt Samantha, y'all shouldn't have gone to so much trouble."

Annie's mom wiped her hands on her apron. "Shawna, this is absolutely no trouble. I'm thrilled to have you here!"

Shawna's face lit up, showing perfect, tiny white teeth.

Annie was amazed her mom could have kept such a gigantic secret from her, even for a day. "Okay. Tell me everything," she demanded.

"Your grandmother called me yesterday morning with the good news that Shawna would be coming to Big Lake *now*, instead of waiting until June." Mom stopped dipping ice cream, and the line tightened around Mick.

"I got homesick and couldn't wait any longer to be here," Shawna explained.

"You were homesick for Big Lake?" Mick asked. "I thought you'd never been here?"

"I mean, I was homesick for America," Shawna said. "I know I'm going to miss Mom and Dad, and maybe even Paris, but my prep school ended last week, and all I could think about was getting back to the US."

"Sweet! Your school's over already?" Storm asked. "In March? Sign me up, man!"

Shawna laughed. "We started in early June."

"June?" Mick repeated. "What about summer baseball?"

"Not sure," Shawna answered. "The French academy I went to rotated quarters. It was pretty strange, but I got my sophomore year in."

"That so rocks!" Storm exclaimed. "Except for the June part."

Annie's stomach knotted every time one of her friends said something to Shawna. She wanted to screen their words first so nothing would get through that might hurt Shawna's feelings, even by accident. "Sounds like a pretty good system to me. I'd start in June if I could get out by March."

"The Paris school was okay, I guess. It was just different from the one I went to back home." Shawna was quiet for a second. "It felt kind of military. It was hard to get to know anybody."

"Is that part of the uniform they made you wear?"

Annie swung around to see who had been rude enough to ask such a question. Bridget, of course. Annie hadn't seen her come in.

Shawna thumbed the collar of her white shirt. She wore it untucked over a pleated navy skirt. "Y'all guessed it. We had to wear our uniforms every day. I have four outfits just like this."

"I could never do that!" Bridget exclaimed. "It would be like denying me half my life."

"You get used to it," Shawna offered.

"Well, I, for one, love your skirt," Annie tried. She could have kicked Bridget for making Shawna feel self-conscious about her clothes. Poor girl hadn't even been in Big Lake a day, and already people were bagging on her about her wardrobe. "I'm going to look for a skirt just like it. And white shirts never go out of style. That one would look so cool with jeans!"

Annie's mind was in spin cycle. She needed to get Shawna a new wardrobe. Annie would have given her anything, including the shirt off her back, but her shirt would have been way too long. Skirts and pants too. She'd figure something out. Annie would do whatever it took to make sure her cousin fit in.

"There she is!" Granny Lind made her entrance, with Gramps behind her. "Everybody treating you all right, sugar?"

Shawna bounced up from her stool and raced to hug her grandparents. "Isn't it crazy that I hadn't seen y'all in years until you picked me up at the airport, but now you've only been gone an hour, and I missed y'all like crazy?"

Gramps touched Shawna's cheek. "You remind me so much of your daddy. Of your uncle too."

Annie stopped breathing. Did Shawna really look like her dad in some way? She wondered if her mom could see it. The only picture Annie had in her mind of Johnny Lind came from the family photo album. And he didn't look much like Shawna.

"I think that's the nicest thing anybody's ever said to me," Shawna declared, throwing her arms around Gramps' neck.

"Sam?" Gramps called over to her. "Are you sure Shawna ought to stay at your place? Granny and I would take real good care of her."

Annie started to object, but her mom beat her to it. "It's all settled, Gramps, and you know it," Mom answered. "I promised Shawna's mother I'd keep her in school with Annie.

Shawna's parents think it will be a good transition back into
the American school system. They want her to keep busy."

"So you'll go to school with me?" Annie couldn't believe
how great this was getting.

Shawna nodded. "Hope that's okay with y'all."

"That's so tight!" Annie exclaimed.

"Shawna can share Annie's room until we turn that den
into another bedroom," Mom explained.

Annie hoped that would take a long time. She pictured
talking with Shawna after they turned out the lights, sharing
secrets and confiding about guys they liked. "You heard
Mom, Gramps. Shawna stays with us! Besides, you couldn't
expect her to keep up with you guys."

"True," Gramps said, winking at Granny.

Granny elbowed him. They were so much in love, even after
all these years. Annie thought *they* should be Professor Love.

"Annie!" Mick called. "I'll work your shift. Why don't you
show your cousin around Big Lake?"

"You sure, Mick?" There was nothing Annie would rather
do. "You're not spent from all that scooping?"

"I'm good." Mick waved the ice-cream scoop at them. "Go!"

Annie led the way, with Storm and Shawna scurrying to
keep up. "I hope you don't hate winter," she began, deciding
to circle the town and end up at her own house. "We still get
snow in March."

"This is my first winter in Big Lake too," Storm said. "Feel
free to call and commiserate. That's *nine-one-one, I-hate-winter*."

"But the snow's gorgeous!" Annie didn't want Shawna
to start out hating Ohio. "Bet you never got snow in New
Orleans."

Shawna shook her head, then shoved her hands in her jacket pockets. Annie made a mental note to get her a warm coat and gloves.

"That Hurricane Katrina must have been something," Storm said. "I read that in ten minutes a hurricane releases more energy than all the nuclear weapons detonated at once. Plus, if you took all the hurricanes — "

"That's Crafts-R-Us across the street," Annie said, cutting off Storm. She figured the last thing her cousin wanted was to talk about hurricanes.

They kept walking up Main Street, with Annie pointing out the sights. When they stopped to peer into the Main Street Diner, four old men frowned out at them.

"Just like those sidewalk cafes in Paris, huh?" Storm joked.

Annie hurried up the street. "This is Farley's Frames. Guess it's the closest thing to a museum in Big Lake. But we're not that far from Cleveland. Jazz — Jasmine Fletcher, one of our friends — is a terrific artist."

"Her cartoons rock!" Storm said.

"Can't wait to meet her," Shawna said. "Hey, do you guys ever go ice fishing?"

"Ice fishing?" Annie didn't like any kind of fishing. Hooks. Worms. What was to like? They headed toward the Old West End.

"I've never been fishing," Shawna continued. "I think it's something I should do at least once. What kind of fish are in Big Lake?"

The only fish Annie knew about were the ones her mom fried for fish sandwiches at Sam's Sammich Shop. "They might do ice fishing on Lake Erie."

"Shawna, I know exactly where you're coming from."
Storm did her walking-backwards thing in front of them.
"Oddly enough, when I moved here, I too was under the
illusion that there must be a big lake in Big Lake, Ohio."

"There's no big lake?" Shawna asked.

"Not even a small lake," Storm answered.

Annie had lived in Big Lake so long that she never
associated her town's name with a real lake. "But we can still
go fishing ... somewhere."

"Mick and Gracie Doe live just up that street," Storm said,
pointing to one of the newer areas of the Old West End.
"You met Mick scooping ice cream. Gracie started our — "
Storm stopped and rephrased. "Gracie is a sophomore like
you and Annie. She's on the school paper too." Storm raised
her eyebrows at Annie, and Annie figured she'd almost said
something about their website or Gracie's blog. Gracie made
them promise to keep it all anonymous.

Annie wondered how she'd be able to keep *That's What
You Think!* a secret from her cousin. She didn't want to have
secrets from her.

The tour continued through the West End. When they
passed Storm's house, she said, "That's my palace. I think it
has the distinction of being the smallest house in town."

"Are those rosebushes?" Shawna asked. She jogged over to
the bare, thorny branches that circled the house.

"My dad has ten green fingers," Storm said.

"You're so lucky!" Shawna exclaimed. "I love flowers.
That's one of the things I miss most about New Orleans."

Annie knew that Shawna couldn't have said anything
better to Storm. Storm used to do everything she could to

keep her friends from seeing her house and meeting her parents. Not anymore, though.

Storm pulled a rubber band from her pocket. As Annie had seen her do dozens of times, she grabbed her long, silky hair into a high ponytail.

"Rats!" Storm's hair came cascading down again. "That's the second rubber band to break on me today."

"If you keep rubber bands in the fridge, they last longer," Shawna offered.

"Yeah?" Storm looked impressed. It didn't often happen that somebody gave a trivia fact to Storm Novelo. "Sweet."

The rest of the tour didn't take long. They stopped at Big Lake Foods, but Gracie waved them away because she had a big line at her checkout. Annie figured Shawna would have the hardest time with Gracie. Gracie liked to keep her circle of friends to a minimum.

"I like your high school," Shawna said as they hiked past the school and veered toward Big Lake Community College.

"Still can't believe you're going to school when you don't have to," Storm commented.

"I have to," Shawna explained. "Part of the deal that let me come here. Besides, I want to. I've missed lots of things about American schools."

"Like American guys?" Annie guessed.

Shawna laughed.

"Are you *keed*-ing, *chérie*? Zee French guys are *magnifique, n'est-ce pas*?" Storm's fake French accent sounded real to Annie.

"Not bad, Storm," said Shawna.

"Anyway, when I can get the car, we'll do the mall," Annie added.

They saved Brookside Park for another, warmer day, and finished up at Annie's house.

"Gramps fixed it up for us," Annie explained as they reached the front door. "Mom never locks up, but don't tell Gramps."

The second Annie opened the door, out bounded Marbles, their shaggy mutt. "Marbles! Here, boy!"

Marbles ignored her and lumbered straight for Shawna. Annie tried to call him back, but he raced at Shawna and jumped, nearly knocking her down. She stumbled and caught her balance. "Hey, fella."

"Marbles, down!" Annie cried.

The dog took off, running circles in the lawn, always finishing at Shawna's feet.

"Looks like you lost your Marbles," Storm observed.

"He's usually shy around strangers," Annie said.

Shawna stroked his shaggy head. "You're a good dog, aren't you, Marbles?"

"Good and slobbery," Storm added, keeping her distance.

"Ah," Shawna said to Marbles, not to Storm, "you can't help panting, can you? You sweat from your feet. So the only way to cool off is to pant. Right?"

"True dat," Storm said, sounding impressed.

"Sorry," Shawna said, lifting Marbles' big, dirty feet from her shoulders and letting the dog down easy. "I'm a trivia buff. Can't help myself."

"Unreal," Storm muttered.

"Storm's into trivia too," Annie said, thrilled that two of her favorite people had so much in common.

Storm raised Annie's wrist and squinted at her watch. "I gotta jet. I need to finish writing something and get Gracie off my back."

"You write too?" Shawna asked. "I'm not much of a writer, but I read a lot. I'd love to read your stuff."

Storm hesitated. "Maybe . . ."

Shawna glanced down at her shoes. "I'm sorry. I don't know you well enough. I shouldn't have asked."

Annie couldn't stand Shawna feeling left out. "Of course, you can read it! Right, Storm? You'd love to let Shawna read your article."

Storm glanced at Annie sideways. "Are you sure? What about — ?"

Annie interrupted her. "Send it to us as soon as you're done. E-mail me." That way, Shawna wouldn't have to know that the article was actually a blog for *That's What You Think!*

"I don't want to force you into anything," Shawna said.

"Are you kidding?" Storm asked. "I've never known anybody besides me who was into trivia. That's what I write mostly. It'll be great having another trivia buff read it. I'll send it over as soon as I'm done."

"Thanks, Storm." Shawna dodged just in time to avert another Marbles' slobber attack.

"No problem." Storm lowered her voice and moved closer to Annie. "No problem for me anyway. I just wouldn't want to be you if Gracie hears about this."

6

The evening flew by. Granny and Gramps came over with a daybed and a chicken casserole. Then they relieved Annie's mom at the shop, and Sam brought Mick home with her. The four of them talked so much during dinner that they barely touched Gran's casserole.

After Mom and Mick went back for closing, Annie and Shawna hung out in Annie's room. As soon as Storm's e-mail arrived, Annie tossed an armful of dirty clothes into the closet to clear another seat at the computer. Then she clicked on the attachment from Storm.

"You don't think Storm minds having me read it?" Shawna asked. "She didn't seem all that sure at first."

"That's just Storm," Annie said. "Come on."

Storm had wisely left off the name of the website and even the name of her own blog, "Didyanose," as in "Did you know."

SUBJECT: YOU THINK YOUR LIFE'S NOT FAIR?
So you don't like your eyes? Your friend has killer blues, big as oceans, and you got blah bullet eyes? Or maybe you hate your ears? Things could be worse. You could be a fish. Did you know:

- *Fish can't blink . . . except for sharks! How come sharks have all the fun?*
- *Nobody — fish or fowl, human or beast — has eyes as big as the eyes of the giant squid. No fair!*
- *Pigs have such short necks and big heads that it's impossible for them to look up into the sky. Talk about unfair!*
- *Cats have 32 muscles in each ear and can move their ears every which way. I can't even wiggle my ears. No fair!*
- *Most dogs have about 100 different facial expressions. But poor bulldogs and pit bulls only have 10 expressions. No wonder they get into so many fights! Nobody understands them.*
- *Talk about unfair! Dogs could die from chocolate. Something in the chocolate sets off a dog's central nervous system and heart muscle. Dogs should never have chocolate. I think I'd die without chocolate!*
- *The people who made the 101 Dalmatians movie tried to be fair and give each puppy exactly 32 spots. But Perdita ended up with 68 and Pongo 72.*
- *Finally, I'll give you one truth that's unfair for everyone. Nobody can lick his or her own elbow.*

Shawna laughed so loud Annie had to cover her right ear. "Storm is spun! Is she on the school paper, like Gracie? Does she always write trivia?"

Annie hated lying to her cousin. "Storm loves to write trivia," she said, dodging the question. "She says it keeps her from spilling out too much in class."

"Exactly! Same with me." Shawna walked over to the bed, Marbles close on her heels. "Annie, I still don't want y'all to give up your bed."

"I'm taking the daybed," Annie insisted. They'd already had this fight. Shawna didn't talk about it, but Annie knew she'd lost her home to Hurricane Katrina. The least Annie could do was give up her bed.

"Well, okay. But if y'all change your mind, the offer stands." Shawna yawned. "It's been a long day. I don't even know what time my body thinks it is."

"Go ahead. You shower first."

"Thanks." Shawna unzipped her suitcase. She only had one bag. Annie couldn't imagine fitting all her stuff into one suitcase. And the Linds weren't exactly well off.

"You're welcome to anything in my closet," Annie offered. "I'm just afraid nothing will fit." She pulled out her favorite flannel nightgown from her bottom drawer. "Maybe this will work." She tossed it to Shawna.

"Thanks! I could have used this in Paris."

"Don't worry about what to wear for school. We'll figure something out. Mom's my size, although her feet are smaller. You know whose clothes would fit you?"

Shawna turned from her suitcase, grinning. "Storm's?"

Annie nodded. "How do you feel about lime green, orange, and purple?"

Shawna laughed. "Perfect. For Storm. I can muddle through with my trusty white shirt."

Annie didn't say anything, but she was already adding up how much she had saved from working at the shop. Not enough.

"Y'all sure it's okay if I shower first?"

"Positive. I have to do stretches anyhow." Since Shawna had shown up, thoughts of the fall had been squeezed out of Annie's mind. Now, they came rushing back.

"Do y'all do exercises every night?" Shawna asked, shoving her suitcase back under the bed.

"Yep. Morning too, unless I'm running late."

"Is that how you stay in shape?"

"I'm trying to get more limber so I can do a heel stretch in cheerleading competition."

Shawna stared at her. "You're a cheerleader? Of course! I should have known."

"Really?" Annie had always thought she looked like a cheerleader, as long as you didn't look at her feet.

"Absolutely! Must be in the genes."

Annie screamed. "You cheer!"

Shawna's smile shrank. "I used to."

Annie didn't know what to say. Shawna's school had closed after the hurricane. "Once a cheerleader, always a cheerleader!"

"My best friend back home used to say, 'Cheerleading sneakers ... $60; Cheerleading camp ... $150; Cheerleading uniform ... $175; Cheering ... priceless!' But it's a lot of work, isn't it?"

Annie laughed. "If it were any easier, they'd call it football."

"You better get to it then."

Annie pushed herself with every stretch. She wanted to feel the pain and let it block out everything else. The phone rang three times, but she let the machine get it. Harder and harder she worked her arms and legs. She dropped into splits, willing herself to meet the ground flat. But it didn't happen.

Shawna walked in, and Annie scurried to her feet.

"Y'all have such long legs," Shawna said, taking her clothes to her suitcase. "Bet you look great in your jumps."

Annie showered and got ready for bed. When she came out of the bathroom, her mom was home, talking to Shawna at the kitchen table. Annie still had a couple of e-mails to answer before she could send off her "Professor Love" blog to Gracie and Mick. She figured this would be the perfect time to do it. Slipping into her bedroom, she closed the door behind her, turned on the computer, and went to work.

Dear Professor Love,

My girlfriend goes ballistic if anyone even mentions my former girlfriend. She keeps asking me how she measures up to my ex. If she's prettier, smarter, funnier, sexier . . . It's like she's competing with her, and it's driving me crazy. What should I do?

— Haunted

Dear Haunted,

Try convincing your girlfriend that she's your girlfriend because she's who she is, not who she's not. Does that make sense? I wish your girlfriend had written in. Sounds like she's fallen victim to chronic comparison. This disease is often fatal to a relationship.

Love, Professor Love

Dear Professor Love,

I need help! My boyfriend likes his buddies better than he likes me! He hangs with them before school, and I have

2 pull him away 2 get him 2 walk me to class. A couple of nights a week he plays basketball with them when he could be seeing me. I know he wants to eat with them at lunch too. How can I compete with guys he's known his whole life? It's not fair!

—Losing fast

Dear Losing,

I'll tell you how you can compete with his buddies ... don't! Let the guys be guys! Don't be jealous of his time with friends. Be glad he has friends, especially if they're good guys. Beware of a guy with no guy friends! And another thing — you need to get along with his friends if you want to be part of his life. Be nice to them, friendly, funny. Don't pretend you're someone you're not, and don't flirt with them or anything! Just respect them and their friendship with your guy.

Love, Professor Love

"Who's Professor Love?"

Annie almost fell off her chair. She hadn't even heard Shawna walk in. She tried to exit the blog, but her fingers fumbled on the keys.

"Wait! Let me finish. This is such a great column. Is it a blog? Do you know who Professor Love is?"

Annie had no idea how to answer. "Well ..."

Shawna stood up and faced the door. "Do *you* know Professor Love?"

Annie peered around her computer, expecting to see her mom standing in the doorway. Instead, there stood Grace Doe, hands on hips, frown on face. Annie couldn't begin to read people's body language the way Gracie did, but it didn't take an expert to read Gracie now. She looked fighting mad.

7

"Gracie? What are you doing here?" Annie realized it was the second time today she'd asked that question. "I mean, I didn't know you were coming."

Gracie didn't say a word.

Shawna looked from Gracie to Annie. "Gracie said you didn't answer your phone, so she came over."

"I turned off my cell," Annie admitted. She didn't mention letting the house phone ring while she did stretches. "Sorry, Gracie." The only reason Gracie would show up at this time of night was to collect the "Professor Love" blog for *That's What You Think!*

Again, Shawna glanced from one to the other as the room filled with tension. "Um ... Gracie, want to see something cool? Annie and I were just looking at 'Professor Love —'"

"That's okay, Shawna," Annie interrupted, feeling things sink from bad to super bad. "Gracie's probably in a hurry. I'll just send you an e-mail with what you wanted. Okay?"

No response, unless you counted the deep sigh.

Annie got the feeling Shawna was trying to make peace. "Hey, Gracie, are y'all writers in Big Lake? You're on the paper. And Storm writes those funny trivia columns."

"She what?" Gracie asked.

Annie's mom walked up behind Gracie. "Everything okay in here? Kind of late, don't you think? We've all got church tomorrow."

Gracie turned her back on Annie and Shawna. "Right. Thanks, Sam. I gotta bounce."

"Gracie?" Annie called.

But it was too late. Gracie disappeared down the hall. Annie heard the door slam after her.

Annie's mom told them good-night and went back to her room.

"Annie, I'm sorry," Shawna said when they were by themselves again. "Did I say something wrong to Gracie?"

"No way!" Annie typed in Gracie's e-mail address and attached the "Professor Love" blog. But she didn't send a friendly note along, the way she usually did. Sure, Grace Doe was a loner. Yeah, Annie and the others had promised Gracie they'd keep *That's What You Think!* anonymous. But that didn't give her the right to be rude to Shawna. "Gracie's hard to get to know. We had classes together for years before we even talked to each other. But once you get to know her, she's really terrific. You'll like her. I promise."

"I already like her," Shawna said. "I just don't think she's crazy about me." She let out a wide yawn that made Annie yawn too.

"Let's get to bed." Annie climbed into the daybed and discovered she wasn't a great fit. Her feet hung over. She bent her knees and tried to get comfortable. "Here, Marbles," she called. It would be a tight fit, but Marbles had slept at the foot of her bed since the day she and Mom had brought him home from the pound.

Marbles trotted over, sniffed the daybed and licked Annie's hand. Then he took off, paws slipping on the floor, and bounded up onto the bed.

"Marbles, no!" Annie shouted. "Come!"

But the shaggy dog stretched out on the bed, his chin on Shawna's chest.

"Hey, Marbles." Shawna stroked his head, and Annie heard the dog's contented groan. "It's okay, Annie. I don't mind at all. In fact, I'd like to sleep with Marbles if y'all are okay with it."

"You sure?" Annie asked.

"We're sure. Aren't we, Marbles?"

"Okay then," Annie said. "Night. Can you reach the lamp?"

The room gave in to darkness without a shimmer of moonlight seeping through the window. Yet even as Annie curled herself under the covers, she wondered if she could get a good night's sleep without her dog. She was so used to having Marbles close and hearing that steady breathing when she woke in the night.

"Annie?" Shawna whispered. "Would it be okay if we prayed together?"

"Sure." Annie wished she'd thought of it herself. She should have. What was wrong with her? She prayed every night before going to sleep. Well, almost every night. Some nights, like tonight, her mind was too filled with other things. When would she ever be like her mom, or Mick? God came first with them, no matter what.

"I can start," Shawna offered. *Father, how can I thank y'all for bringing me here, for how nice Annie is to share her room with me? Thanks for Aunt Sam. And Granny and Gramps Lind. And thanks for Marbles and knowing he's just what I need right now. Y'all are too much, Lord! Will you look out for Mama and Daddy, please?*

Make sure Mama remembers to wear her scarf. Help Daddy not to get discouraged when not many show up for services. On the other hand, why don't you just get more people to those services?

Shawna prayed for people her parents served as missionaries. Annie could tell by her voice that she really cared about the ministry, that she'd been part of it. Her prayers were more like talking to God, the way Mick prayed, so natural Annie wouldn't have been surprised to look up and see Jesus listening. Shawna prayed for Annie's friends too. Annie loved listening to her. She fell asleep to Shawna's conversation with God.

Annie woke to a pounding on her door. "Annie! This is your last call! Up and at 'em right now!"

Annie shook herself awake. Her legs felt cramped. She scrambled out of bed. Only her foot wouldn't move. The rest of her plopped back, half on the bed, half off. Her face would have slammed the floor if she hadn't caught herself. Her foot was stuck between the bars at the end of her bed, the daybed. She had to twist her foot and pull it out before she could crumble in a pile onto the floor. Marbles trotted over and licked her face. Annie's brain cleared, and everything came back to her.

Shawna.

Annie glanced around the room. No sign of her cousin. The bed looked like it hadn't been slept in. "Shawna?" she hollered.

Marbles barked, as if agreeing with her.

Annie scurried to the hall. "Shawna?"

Mom stuck her head out of her bedroom. She was wearing her brown suit with a silk shirt and makeup. "I'm leaving for church in fifteen minutes, with or without you."

"Where's Shawna?"

"Already there, I'd imagine. Gran and Gramps brought over breakfast, which you slept through. They took Shawna to church with them."

"Without me?" This was a class-A felony. What did Shawna wear? Who would she sit with? Plus, Annie had planned to mediate between Shawna and Gracie. What if they ran into each other before she got there?

"You had your chance to go with them, and you slept through it." Mom glanced at her watch. "Now you have thirteen minutes before the last buggy heads out of Dodge."

Annie had never dressed so fast. She didn't even put on lipstick. Why should she worry about how she looked when she went to church? On the other hand, Dallas from Middleview would be there — extremely hot and dreamy Dallas. Just friends for now, but who knew about later? There was no way she had time to wash her hair, so she brushed it back in a mini-ponytail.

"This minute, Annie!" Mom called upstairs.

Annie gave her hair one last flounce and ran out.

As they drove to church, Annie prayed silently: *Father, I'm not there to look out for Shawna, so will you please look out for her? Talk to Gracie and make her be nice to my cousin. I really want everybody to like Shawna.*

She ran into church before her mom had time to shut off the engine. The piano music stopped. The pews seemed pretty full as the pastor got up to make announcements. Annie spotted Gran and Gramps, but Shawna wasn't with them.

Then she saw Gracie in the pew behind Gramps. Next to Gracie sat Shawna, with Storm and Mick on her other side. Annie waved, but they didn't seem to see her.

"Annie, over here!" Her mother motioned for Annie to take one of the few empty seats on the back row.

From where she sat, Annie could keep an eye on Shawna and Gracie. They shared a hymnal. Once Annie thought she caught them passing a note back and forth. She tried to pay attention to the service, but she couldn't help counting the minutes until church ended and she could meet up with everybody in the youth group room.

As soon as she could, Annie made her way through the crowd and took the stairs down to her classroom. She heard laughter. Then she recognized Shawna's voice.

"And I said, 'Sorry y'all, but I don't speak French.'"

The room exploded in laughter as Annie walked in.

"There's Annie!" Storm waved her over. She was sitting with Gracie and Shawna, but there wasn't an empty seat anywhere around them.

Shawna glanced to her right, then her left. "Well, shoot! I wanted to save y'all a seat, Annie. Maybe I should say that Storm and I were saving you a seat. But then Miss Gracie came over. And y'all know what a bully she is."

Gracie elbowed Shawna. "Shut up." But she was laughing.

Annie shook her head in disbelief. It had taken her years to be able to joke with Gracie.

"Use your attic," Storm whispered, tapping her head. "The only empty seat is next to Dallas. You go, girl!"

Annie made a face at her, then slipped into the empty seat. Dallas looked so hot in khakis, a navy polo shirt, and dark sunglasses, although she couldn't figure out why he still had the sunglasses on. "Hey, Dallas. What's with the cheaters?"

"Forgot my regular glasses," Dallas explained. "These are prescription." He leaned closer, and Annie felt his arm press against hers. "Do you know her?"

"Who?"

"*Her.* The really hot girl next to Storm. Where did she come from?"

"Paris. And New Orleans." Annie wasn't sure why, but she'd started not enjoying this conversation. "She's my cousin, Dallas. She's staying with me."

"Will you introduce me?" He tore his gaze from Shawna and faced Annie with his biggest grin. "Please, Annie. I have to meet her."

"You bet, Dallas," she answered sweetly. She'd have to reevaluate Dallas Hughes. Hitting on the new girl in church was pretty out of order. Very uncool. Annie might have been smiling at him on the outside.

Inside, Annie was not smiling.

8

After church, Annie kept her promise and introduced Dallas to her cousin.

"Are ya'll from Texas?" Shawna asked.

"Nah. I've lived in Ohio my whole life."

Shawna laughed. "Y'all know how to fool a girl. Big Lake without a lake. Now Dallas without Texas."

The girls headed outside, but Dallas caught up with them on the church lawn.

"I go to Middleview High School." He almost stumbled over himself trying to get next to Shawna. "It's just a couple miles down the road. I could show you around sometime."

"Thanks, Dallas," Shawna said. Annie couldn't tell if that meant yes or no.

"We play Big Lake in basketball this week. Maybe I'll see you there?"

Shawna smiled. "Maybe."

Annie started toward Mom's car, and Shawna and Gracie followed. Storm skipped a circle around Shawna, chanting, "He likes you. He likes you."

"Storm, be two, will you?" Gracie scolded.

Annie changed the subject. "So what's up with you, Gracie? Last night you acted like my cousin had come to Big Lake as an enemy spy. This morning you're giggling together in church?"

"Guess I changed my mind about her."

"Just like that?" Annie asked. Grace Doe rarely changed her mind about anything.

Gracie shrugged. "This morning I got to know Shawna."

"This morning?" It had taken Annie years to get Gracie to return a smile.

"I helped," Storm interjected. "I told Gracie Shawna was filled with grooviness."

"And in spite of that, I gave her a chance," Gracie teased. "I could tell by her body language that she's for real."

"Turns out we both like Sherlock Holmes." Shawna waved to someone in the parking lot. "Gracie likes the way he picks up on clues everybody else misses."

"Sweet," Annie muttered. This is exactly what she'd wanted. Her cousin had made friends with Annie's friends. She just hadn't expected it to happen so fast.

Gracie left with her own family. Storm waited with Annie and Shawna.

Mom walked out with Gran. "How did you like church?" Gran asked.

"I loved it!" Shawna answered. "Maybe later we can talk about how I can get involved in things."

"That would be great!" Annie's mom said. "We could talk over lunch."

"Actually, I was going to ask if y'all minded if I went home with Storm for lunch."

"With Storm?" Annie asked.

"You can come too if you want, Annie," Storm offered. "I thought Shawna could thumb through my closet. See if anything fits."

"That's nice of you, Storm," Mom answered. "You kids have fun."

Annie thought about joining them. But she didn't want to get in the way. Storm and Shawna seemed to be getting along great. "I need to practice the new cheers this afternoon. Good luck clothes hunting."

Since it was just the two of them for lunch, Annie made tuna sandwiches. While her food settled, she logged onto *That's What You Think!* to read Gracie's blog. As usual, Mick had posted a verse to go along with the blog theme.

• •

THAT'S WHAT YOU THINK!

VERSE OF THE WEEK

> *"Friend, I am not being unfair to you . . . Don't I have the right to do what I want with my own money? Or are you envious because I am generous!"*
>
> —Matthew 20:13, 15

by Jane
MARCH 11
SUBJECT: NO FAIR!

Today at work I listened for two little words I hear all the time in the halls of Typical High: No fair! Kids say this when they get their grades. Entire classes shout "No fair!" in unison when the teacher announces *a pop quiz. Who doesn't think "No fair!" when it snows on the weekend but melts by Monday, robbing us of snow days?*

I thought I'd be lucky to catch "No fair!" once or twice. Instead, I heard those exact words half a dozen times, and that doesn't count body language (pursed lips, sudden intake of air, stiffening of shoulders, straightening of back).

When a businesswoman realized her line moved slower than others, she fumed at the unfairness. An older man told anyone who would listen that he'd gotten gas in the morning, and they'd lowered the price a nickel in the afternoon. No fair. A college student couldn't stop complaining to her friend that the coat she'd bought at 20% off was now on sale for 70% off. "It's not fair!" she insisted.

Oddly enough, not one person complained how unfair it was when her line moved fastest. Or when he got something at a better price than someone else. I've never heard a Typical High student gripe about getting a good grade he didn't deserve. But isn't that as unfair as the other way around?

Think about it. . . .

Annie loved Gracie's blogs. She wished she could show this one to Shawna. But that would probably wreck the good relationship they were developing.

Before heading outside to practice cheers, Annie rang Storm to check on the clothes hunt.

Storm's mother answered. "She's not here. Storm and that sweet girl, Shawna, went out. It's such a beautiful day."

Annie felt more disappointed than she should have. She changed into sweats, then decided to see what Gracie was up to. Annie dialed Gracie's house, and Mick answered. "Hi, Mick."

"Hey, Annie! What's up?"

"Not much. I'm getting ready to practice cheer routines. Is Gracie around?"

"Nope. Storm called looking for wardrobe possibilities for Shawna. I think Gracie ran some stuff over to them."

"Cool," Annie said. "Thanks." She started to hang up, but changed her mind. "Mick, are you doing anything?"

"Nothing much. Ty went somewhere with his family."

"You want to come over? I'm working on the cheerleading competition routine. Maybe you can help."

"Sure. Don't know how much help I'll be, though. See you in a few minutes."

When Mick got there, they found a spot in the backyard out of the wind. First, Annie showed Mick the new welcome cheer the squad would do Tuesday. She made two mistakes and had to start over. "Mick, let me teach you this one. Our coach says teaching a cheer is the best way to learn it."

Mick went along with the plan, even though Annie knew she'd never go out for cheerleading. Mick would rather play the sport than cheer it. After two tries, Mick had it down perfectly.

"You got that a lot faster than I did," Annie admitted.

"I doubt it. Besides, I could never pull it off in front of a crowd like you do."

Annie explained stunting to Mick. "Let me show you the Liberty."

"You okay?" Mick asked.

Annie wasn't okay. She couldn't explain why her heart pounded just thinking about the stunt. She had to press past this. "C'mon. I'll show you how it works. The bases lift me up on one leg." She sprang as high as she could, keeping one leg straight, the other tucked.

"Annie! The Lib! I love the Lib!" Shawna came jogging up with Storm close behind. Shawna wore a screaming red skirt with a white shirt, sleeves rolled up. Not bad, especially considering the source.

"The Lib?" Storm asked, not looking impressed.

"The Liberty!" Shawna explained. "Y'all looked great, Annie!"

"You think?" Annie didn't feel so great.

"Excuse me while I go somewhere and hurl," Storm said.

"Storm Novelo," Shawna scolded, "don't tell me y'all are down on cheerleading?"

"*Moi*? What could I possibly have against jumping around in short skirts and yelling in public, not to mention risking life and limb for it?"

"Life and limb?" Annie asked.

"Apparently, you haven't seen the stats on the fine art of cheerleading," Storm said.

"I have," Shawna countered. "Cheerleading is the number-one female sport in high school."

"It's the number-one sport," Storm agreed, "for female catastrophic injuries. More than half the chick injuries in high school athletics are down to cheerleading. Did you know you're more likely to be hurt being tossed in the air as a cheerleader than you are being tackled on the football field?"

"Is that true?" Annie asked. This wasn't helping.

"True dat!" Storm insisted.

"So what are you saying?" Shawna demanded. "That Annie should quit cheering?"

"Now why would I say that?" Storm asked. "I mean, why would I want a friend of mine to stop flirting with serious injury?"

Mick had been staring, statue still, as Storm spouted her statistics. Now she turned to Annie. "Annie, did you know all this?"

"Annie doesn't care about statistics, Mick!" Shawna insisted. "Right, Annie?"

"Right." But she kept going back to what Storm said about football tackles versus cheerleading tosses.

"Well, I'll leave you to your follies," Storm said. "Promised Dad I'd help in the garden."

"Tell him thanks again for the gardening lesson," Shawna said.

Storm grinned, and Annie could tell how pleased she was. "Dad loved talking flowers with you. Gotta bounce."

"Bye, Storm," Mick said.

As soon as Storm was out of sight, Shawna sighed. "I miss cheering."

"I hear you," Annie said. "I don't know what I'd do without cheering. I've cheered every year, although this is my first year as flyer."

"You're a flyer? Man, you must be great to be so tall and still fly!"

"Not all that great," Annie admitted.

"Are you kidding?" Mick said. "Shawna, you should see the faces Annie makes when she's up there! Me and my friends go to games just to watch Annie."

Annie grinned at Mick. The Munch always seemed to know what to say. Annie loved the making-faces part of flying. In competition, she had to work her facial expressions to show excitement and surprise as the tumblers did their routines. Some flyers stuck out their tongues and crossed their eyes, but Annie went for wide-eyed amazement.

"I was never good at faces," Shawna said. "I'd love to see you at work, Annie."

"You will!" Mick exclaimed. "There's a game Tuesday."

"That's right," Shawna said. "The one with Middleview, or whatever Dallas's team is called."

Annie loved cheering games. It would be great to have Shawna there.

"I better get going," Mick said. "Have to help Mom with the twins."

"Your mom has twins?" Shawna asked.

Mick nodded. "Two-year-olds."

"You're so lucky, Mick. Gracie and twins."

"And Luke. My big brother."

"Her extremely cute big brother," Annie added. Luke was two years older than Gracie and Annie. Like half the girls at BLHS, Annie had always had a little crush on Luke.

After Mick left, Shawna and Annie stayed outside and talked cheerleading. "So what's your favorite stunt?" Shawna asked.

"Toe touches," Annie answered.

"Those are fun, aren't they?" Shawna agreed.

"And the Lib."

"Gotta love the Lib."

"I've been working on heel stretches." Annie kicked her leg as far up as she could.

"You almost did it, Annie. With those legs of yours, y'all could reach the sky flying."

"How about you?" Annie asked.

"I haven't done much since New Orleans." Shawna stood on her toes, then squatted, then stretched. "Not the best skirt for the job." Suddenly, she kicked her leg straight above her head and held it in a perfect heel stretch.

"Man! How did you do that?"

"I'm pretty rusty. But I can show you the way my coach in New Orleans taught us to do it."

"Yeah?"

"Hey, what are cousins for?"

For the next hour, Shawna helped Annie work on the heel stretch. When Shawna did it, she made it look easy. Annie got better, but she couldn't kick high enough.

"I think you got it that time!" Shawna shouted.

"But did I get my heel up high enough?" Annie was so beat she couldn't tell.

"If you'd been lifted in the Elevator, you'd have nailed it. You should go for it."

Annie could picture herself in the competition, pulling the stunt on her last Elevator rise. It would be so fly. "Ms. Whitney, our coach, would freak."

"What's she like?"

"You can meet her in practice after school tomorrow if you want."

"I'd love to watch practice."

Annie's mom stuck her head out the back door and shouted, "Shawna! Your mom's on the phone."

Shawna took off at a dead run. She was so fast Annie thought she could easily make it on the Big Lake track team. She watched Shawna run full-speed all the way to the house.

All Annie could do was shake her head and wonder if there was anything her cousin couldn't do.

Monday when Annie woke up, Shawna wasn't there. Annie stumbled out of the daybed and dashed to the hall. "Mom! Where is she?"

"Down here, Annie!" Shawna yelled back. "Your mom made pancakes."

It took Annie a long time to get ready for school. Her hair didn't cooperate. Then she changed her mind, which meant changing her clothes. By the time she got downstairs, it was time to go.

"Annie," Mom said, stacking her dishes in the sink, "why don't you drive Shawna to school today?"

"Seriously?" Annie had given up begging her mom for the car on school mornings.

"I think it would be nice for you girls to drive on Shawna's first day." Mom smiled at Shawna.

"Aunt Sam, y'all don't have to do this on my account. I love to walk."

"Never argue with Mom," Annie advised. "Trust me. If we leave now, you can meet some people before classes." She kissed her mom good-bye, and Shawna did the same.

On the drive to school, Annie started thinking about cheerleading practice. The closer they got to BLHS, the darker her thoughts. Usually, she couldn't wait for practice. But a sense of dread had set in, and she couldn't shake it. She wondered if her cousin had ever gone through this. "Shawna, did you ever fall when you cheered?"

"All the time! Once I had a bad fall. The spotters were guy watching, I think. Anyway, I crashed. Banged up my ankle like y'all wouldn't believe."

"What did you do?"

"Got back on the horse, if you know what I mean."

"You just got back up?"

"And it was fine. Why are you asking, Annie?"

"No reason." Annie was glad she'd asked. All she needed was to "get back on the horse."

She took a parking spot in the back of the underclassmen lot. "Glad you don't mind walking," she told Shawna as they climbed out of the car. "I love to drive, but I'm still not crazy about parking."

"But you're driving, Annie." Shawna threaded between two red cars. "I don't even have my permit yet."

Annie spotted a group of sophomore girls ahead. "Guys! Wait up!"

Before they even got to Annie's locker, Shawna had met a dozen kids.

"There's Gracie," Shawna said as Annie pulled down books and loaded her pack for morning classes. "What's she doing? Taking notes?"

Gracie jotted her observation notes before school. It was where she got material for her blog on *That's What You Think!* But this wasn't something Annie was free to share.

They walked up to Gracie just as Jazz handed her a sheet of paper. "There. All done," she said.

"Jazz!" Annie called. "I want you to meet my cousin. Shawna, this is Jasmine Fletcher, also known as Jazz. Jazz, this is my cousin, the one I told you about."

"I know. Hi." Jazz could be a woman of few words. She was wearing a sleek brown shirt with black jeans. Annie didn't think the outfit would have worked on anybody but Jazz. Yet it worked perfectly on her. Jazz had probably designed and made the shirt too.

Shawna sidled over toward Gracie and tried to peek at the paper Jazz had given her. "You're the artist, right?"

Annie could tell Jazz liked being known as the artist. "I guess."

"Could I see what you drew?" Shawna reached for the paper.

Gracie yanked it away.

"Gracie!" Shawna demanded, one hand on her hip, the other held out for the paper. "Now, Gracie."

Gracie shrugged and handed it over.

Jazz laughed. "Okay. Who is this pushover, and what have you done with the real Gracie?"

Annie laughed too. She'd never seen stubborn Grace Doe give in so easily.

Suddenly, Shawna burst into laughter that didn't go with her petite body. She snorted and howled so loud people in the hall turned to stare. "Jazz, this is so funny!"

Annie took the paper from Shawna. It was one of Jazz's cartoons, no doubt for the website. Four little kids stood outside a door as a lady doled out Halloween candy. Three of the kids had typical Halloween costumes: a witch, a tiger, and a pirate. The fourth girl wore a skirt, blouse, and suit jacket. The woman of the house was leaning down and asking the regularly dressed kid, "And what are you dressed as, little girl?" The girl answered, "I'm dressing up as my mother and criticizing what everybody else is wearing."

Annie knew Jazz was in continual battle with her mother, a classy, rich lawyer, who wanted her daughter to be something more practical than a starving artist. "It's hilarious, Jazz."

"Yeah," Gracie agreed, no hint of a smile. "Only news flash: It's March, not October thirty-first."

Jazz snatched back the paper and tucked it into her portfolio. "Picky, picky, picky."

"I need something good for March. By tonight. Okay, Jazz?" Gracie said.

"Is it for the paper?" Shawna asked. "Do y'all do cartoons for the school paper?"

Annie glanced from Jazz to Gracie. Then, thankfully, the bell rang. "Better bounce! See you guys later."

It was funny to watch guys flock around Shawna in each class. Liam sat by her and acted like he'd known her for years. "Y'all can't understand what it's like to be a southerner in a northern land. Shawna, you and I have to stick together."

By lunchtime, it was as if everybody in the whole school knew Shawna. Annie had no worries about her cousin fitting in. She sat across from Shawna and eavesdropped on her conversation with Jazz.

"Would you have time, Jazz?" Shawna was saying.

"I wouldn't have offered if I didn't," Jazz answered.

"Time for what?" Annie took a bite of her school taco. It was too soggy. She wished she'd gotten salad like Shawna.

Shawna squeezed a packet of dressing onto her salad. "Jazz said she'd help me turn a pair of my jeans — "

"Or two," Jazz interrupted.

"Into skirts! Isn't that tight?"

"If anybody can do it, Jazz can," Annie commented, wrapping up her soggy taco for the nearest trash bin.

"It's easy," Jazz explained. "You just cut off the bottom of your jeans, separate the legs, and use the leg part to fill in front and back. We can do something cool to style them — embroidery or macramé. I've got paints that work too. If you bring a T-shirt, we can tie-dye."

"I'll come by as soon as cheerleading practice is over," Shawna promised. "Thanks, Jazz."

Annie started to thank Jazz too. Then it seemed silly. Jazz wasn't helping out for Annie's sake. She was doing it for Shawna.

"Wait a minute." Storm broke off her conversation with Gracie and turned to Shawna. "I thought you and I were hitting Goodwill this afternoon."

"That's right. Sorry. I forgot."

While Shawna worked out her social calendar, Annie got up and dumped her lunch. For some reason, she'd lost her appetite.

10

At the end of the day, Shawna and Annie made their way through the crowded, noisy halls to the gym. Annie tried to ignore the queasiness in her stomach. She told herself it was the taco's fault and had nothing to do with her fall.

Rakiah met them at the door. "Good! I was hoping you'd come to practice with Annie."

A couple of the other girls came over. It looked like Shawna had already met most of the cheerleaders. Annie introduced her to Ms. Whitney, but she seemed to be in a rush to get started.

"I'll sit over there out of the way," Shawna said, heading for the bleachers.

"Places, girls!" Ms. Whitney clapped her hands. "We're going through the dance routine until we get it right. Perfect! Got it?"

Annie felt like the question was aimed at her, so she nodded and got in line for the routine. She started strong, with steps and turns coming automatically. Each time she glimpsed Shawna on the bleachers, Shawna was bobbing in time. When they finished, Shawna burst into applause.

Ms. Whitney was less enthusiastic. "Let's do it again. This time everybody smile!"

Annie felt pretty sure this comment wasn't directed at her. Smiling was the one thing she never worried about when she cheered. They ran through the routine again. But halfway through, Annie lost the beat.

"Stop! Annie, count in your head. Everybody, take it from the top!"

Bridget and a couple of the others groaned. Annie felt terrible. She hated it when she made everybody start over. They ran through it again. She knew she'd made at least one mistake. But nobody said anything.

"Take five, people!" Ms. Whitney called. "Don't sit down. Do your stretches. We'll tumble next, with the Elevator behind." The Elevator was the stunt Annie and the bases pulled while the rest of the cheerleaders tumbled. The bases tossed or lifted Annie. Each time she rose, she struck a different pose — a toe touch first, finishing with the Liberty.

Annie tried to shut out thoughts of the Elevator and concentrate on stretching. When she glanced over at the bleachers, she saw a few of the girls gathered around Shawna. After a minute, Shawna laughed. Then Bridget and Callie stepped back and did back handsprings. Bridget said something, and then Callie pulled Shawna to her feet.

Annie moved in to see what was going on.

Shawna was shaking her head. "Y'all, I haven't done one in almost a year."

Rakiah walked up to Annie. "You talk her into it, Annie."

"Into what?"

Bridget smirked over at Annie. "Into doing a back tuck. A *standing* tuck. Unless your cousin was just kidding us."

Annie stared at Shawna. "Can you do a tuck?" None of
the Sharks cheerleaders had pulled it off. They did back
handsprings, landing on hands before feet. In a tuck, you
flipped backwards from a standstill. No hands.

"I used to do tucks," Shawna admitted.

"Then do it!" Bridget insisted.

Annie whispered to Shawna, "Don't let her talk you into
anything."

Shawna let herself be pulled out to the floor. "I'll give it
a shot, y'all. But I may embarrass myself to tears. Or y'all
might have to dial *nine-one-one*." She shook out her arms and
legs. "Here goes nothin'." She tilted forward, then sprang
backward, thrusting her legs straight over her head. As soon
as she landed, she charged the mat into a round-off back
handspring with full twisting layout.

The girls cheered.

"A full!" Ms. Whitney exclaimed. "Shawna, where did you
learn to do a full?"

Shawna shrugged. Her cheeks glowed pink. "Most of us
did tucks in Louisiana competitions. A couple of us did fulls.
I'm surprised I can still do one."

"I knew southern cheerleading was further along than ours,
but I had no idea." Ms. Whitney glanced from the mat to
Shawna. "That was a treat."

"Thank you, ma'am." Shawna took her seat again, but the
other girls followed her, shooting questions from all sides.

"What else can you do?" Callie asked.

Annie figured it was time to join in. "She does a great heel
stretch."

"So does Annie!" Shawna insisted.

Rakiah elbowed Annie. "You didn't tell me you were working on a heel stretch!"

"I don't — " she started.

"It's straight kickin' with those long legs of hers," Shawna said.

"Then you should do it in competition," Bridget said.

"Don't rush her, girls," said their coach. "It would be great if you could do a heel stretch, Annie. But let's concentrate on doing what we know we can do without errors. We'll have time to work on other stunts."

They lined up. Annie always felt like icing on the cake during the tumbling routine. All eyes would be on her when she popped up in the Elevator, no matter what else was going on. Concentrating, she stepped into Callie's and Bridget's hands and felt Sasha and Rakiah close in. They lifted her shoulder height. She made faces, acting surprised by the tumblers she watched from on high.

Down she went, dropping into the "basket" of her bases' arms. Bases dipped, then popped Annie high into the air. She straddled her legs and reached for her toes. Toe touches were her *thing*. They repeated the lifts, with Annie doing different faces each time.

"Great faces, Annie!" Shawna shouted.

Annie dropped into the "basket" then made herself go stiff as they lifted her on one foot for the Liberty. Everything was going all right. Yet she wasn't enjoying it as much as usual. She couldn't get the thought out of her head that her cousin would have been pulling better stunts.

"That's it for today!" Ms. Whitney called. She gave them the rundown for the next day's game and practice times for the week.

As soon as Shawna could break away from Bridget and Callie, she and Annie headed home. Annie waited until they were by themselves. "Why didn't you tell me you could stunt like that?"

"I didn't know if I still could. I could never do faces the way you do. That's a big part of competition now."

Annie knew Shawna was trying to make her feel better. It wasn't working. "I'd give anything if I could do a full. Or a tuck. Or even a heel stretch in the Elevator."

"Annie, you're almost there. If you can do the heel stretch on the ground, you can do it in the air."

"I don't know. I'm starting to agree with Bridget. I'm just too tall to be a flyer."

Shawna stopped. "Listen to me, Annie. I'll admit that when you told me you were a flyer, I couldn't believe anyone your height could pull it off. But you do! They just don't toss you high enough."

High enough? Lately, Annie had felt like every toss sent her *too* high. "Shawna, have you ever been afraid?"

Shawna grew quiet. Annie glanced over at her and was about to repeat the question when Shawna nodded.

Something inside Annie unclenched. If Shawna the amazing cheerleader had felt fear, then maybe what she herself had been feeling all week was normal. "You're not just saying that to make me feel better? *You've* been afraid?"

"Try *terrified*."

"Was it after you fell?" Annie wanted details. "Were you afraid of flying?"

Shawna squinted up at Annie. "Flying? Never! I loved every minute in the air. I fell, but who doesn't?"

"But you said you were afraid — "

"Not when I was cheering. Is that what y'all meant?"

Annie wished she'd never brought up the subject. Shawna had no idea what she was feeling. "It's not important."

"Annie, don't be afraid of the heel stretch. We'll work on it. You'll get it."

Annie wanted to believe her. She'd never felt more awkward than she did right now. Shawna had the skills and natural ability — and small feet. But if she, Annie Lind, could pull a heel stretch in the Elevator, that might make up for just about everything.

11

After dinner Shawna said she needed to run to the library. Annie holed up in her room and worked on homework. Then she thumbed through the e-mails for Professor Love. She was working on a new "Professor Love" column when Shawna walked in with the whole blog team.

"Look who I brought!" Shawna exclaimed as if the girls were a gift to Annie. Shawna wore cool embroidery-laced jeans, the denim cut just below the knee, with bric-brac on the ends. Her macramé belt finished the Jazz original.

Annie didn't know why she had to force herself to smile at them. She loved it when anybody dropped in, especially these guys. Yet something like sandpaper rubbed against the sides of her throat.

"Did we interrupt something?" Mick asked.

Annie scooted back in her desk chair. "Are you knicked out, Mick? You know I love interruptions of any kind, especially the human variety."

Storm plopped on Annie's bed and kicked off her high-topped purple sneakers. They perfectly matched the purple streak in her hair. "Look up *people person* in the dictionary, and there's a picture of Annie."

"True dat!" Annie agreed.

Gracie wriggled out of her army jacket and approached the computer. "What were you working on?"

Annie tried to give Gracie *the look* to warn her that it was blog stuff, things they didn't want to discuss around Shawna. "Nothing much," she answered, raising her eyebrows again in case Gracie still hadn't gotten the message. "Let me exit out of this ..." She began logging off, but Gracie stopped her with a hand over the mouse.

"It's okay. Go ahead and read what you've got so far," Gracie said.

Annie glared at her. "I don't think that's such a good idea. Do you?"

Shawna hustled over to the computer and squeezed in front of Gracie. "Is this a new 'Professor Love' column? Read it, Annie! Please? I LOVE the stuff y'all write. It's so tight!"

"You know?" Annie waited for Gracie to explode. It didn't happen.

"We told her," Gracie said simply.

"You what?"

Jazz had been flipping through a photo album Annie had out on the dresser. She slapped it shut. "Mutual decision."

"Fo' sho'," Storm agreed. She stretched out on the bed, arms locked behind her head. "Your cousin is so filled with grooviness. We were trying on shoes at the thrift store, and I couldn't keep 'Didyanose' a secret from her any longer. So I called Gracie and Mick."

"And we called Jazz," Mick added.

"And we met at the shop over ice cream," Jazz said, "and talked through pros and cons."

"And, like, there weren't any cons," Storm explained. "We knew you'd be down with it. So we filled her in on *That's What You Think!*"

"And swore her to secrecy." Gracie narrowed her eyes at Shawna.

"Gracie made me promise that if I ever gave up the secret, I'd have to give her my firstborn child," Shawna teased.

"That is so federal," Storm said, yawning. "Wrong, wrong, wrong in so many ways."

"I wasn't *that* bad," Gracie countered.

They exchanged one-liners for a few minutes, laughing hysterically. Annie felt out of the loop, something that didn't happen very often. At least it gave her time to soak in the information. Annie was glad they'd told Shawna about their anonymous website. Of course she was. She hadn't liked hiding things from her cousin. Still, it was hard to understand how they'd all come to the conclusion so easily. Without her. Annie would have bet her last tube of lipstick that Grace Doe would *never* divulge her secret identity to anyone else.

"So?" Shawna wrinkled her nose at Annie.

"Sorry. What?"

"Read it!" Shawna commanded. "Or are you going to make me beg?"

Annie snapped herself out of it. "Okay. Professor Love is blazin', but she's only gotten one e-mail answered so far. Here goes." Annie read the question and her answer out loud, while the others settled onto the beds or on the floor.

Dear Professor Love,

I don't know how to tell my best friend, B.J., that she's being totally ditzoid over a guy. She's come on to him all year, and now the poor guy has caved and asked her to a school gig, probably to get her off his back. But B.J. is acting like this is a romance novel, and she's the heroine. She's gone postal, dude! She goes to school with all her bling sparkling, just in case she might run into Mr. Wonderful.

How can I keep my friend from making a total fool of herself?

—D.C.

Dear D.C.,

B.J. is lucky to have a friend who cares as much as you seem to. Sounds as if she may be asking for a big letdown. Before it gets worse, maybe you can give her Professor Love's translation of guy-speak:

- *"I think of you as my little sister." (Meaning: I'm definitely not interested in you as girlfriend material.)*
- *"I'm concentrating on school right now." (Meaning: Get lost.)*
- *"I try never to date where I work or go to school." (See above.)*
- *"I've got a girlfriend." (And it's not you.)*
- *"I'm just not attracted to you in 'that' way." (Meaning: Stop blinging me. It's not working.)*
- *"It's not you. It's me." (Meaning: I really think it's you.)*
- *"Let's just be friends." (Sure.)*

Annie felt kind of bad about the last answer. She'd probably change it before handing the blog to Mick. In the past two months Annie had actually told several guys that she just wanted to be friends. And she'd meant exactly what she said. God had been teaching her how to have boys as friends without having to have boyfriends. The truth was, Annie didn't really believe a lot of the translations in Professor Love's answer to D.C. She was going for the laugh.

She got it too. At least from the blog team. Storm laughed so hard her eyes watered.

"Not bad," Gracie said.

Jazz had a great laugh, and Annie didn't think she used it enough. But she was taking advantage of it now. "Do you think some guy honestly tried that line about not dating anyone where he goes to school?"

Annie turned to Shawna, expecting to hear her unique horse laugh. Instead, her cousin was staring at the computer screen. "You know ...," she began, and the room grew quiet. "I'm probably way off. But I'm thinking D.C. is the one with the problem. Not her friend."

"What do you mean?" Gracie asked, closing in on the screen again.

"Well, what if that guy asked B.J. out because he likes her? Maybe he wants to spend time with her. How would D.C. know, right?"

"That's true," Jazz said.

Annie felt like she needed to defend her answer. "What about all the bling she wears to school to impress the guy?"

"Maybe she does and maybe she doesn't," Shawna answered. "I guess what I'm saying is that I think D.C. might like the guy too."

"And she's jealous!" Storm declared. "She wishes the guy had asked *her*. Right on!"

"But we don't know ..." Annie tried.

"Makes sense," Gracie agreed.

"Nice deduction for a Southern belle," Jazz conceded.

Mick put her arm around Shawna's shoulder. "Shawna, you're right. That poor girl is jealous and doesn't even know it."

"What should we do?" Jazz asked.

"Your verse, Mick!" Storm shouted. "Type it in."

Mick smiled at Annie. "I don't want to take over. Annie knows what she's doing."

"Then just tell her the verse again," Storm urged. "The one you posted to go with our 'No fair!' theme. What was it, Mick?"

"You know the one, Annie," Mick said. "These workers get upset because, even though they got paid a good wage, the guys who didn't work as long got the same pay. It's from Matthew 20. And when they griped about it being unfair that a guy who works all day and a guy who works an hour get paid the same, Jesus told them, *'Friend, I am not being unfair to you ... Don't I have the right to do what I want with my own money? Or are you envious because I am generous!'*"

Storm bounced off the bed as if the bedsprings had sprung. "Yeah! That's the one! Those guys were all happy about getting a job and good money until they found out the other

groups got paid the same thing. They were jealous. Put that
one in, Annie!"

They all agreed. Even Annie could see it, now that Shawna
had pointed it out. D.C. was jealous of her friend. The best
thing Annie could do was to help her see her own envy. "I'll
rework it. Thanks, everybody."

"In the meantime," Mick said, taking control of the
keyboard and clicking to the *That's What You Think!* website,
"you guys have to see the cartoon Jazz gave me."

"Big Chief Gracie wouldn't let me use my Halloween
cartoon," Jazz explained. "So I tried to come up with
something to fit the 'No fair!' theme."

Mick clicked keys at the approximate speed of light then
scooted back so they could see the screen.

The picture showed an empty fairgrounds littered with
remnants of cotton candy, paper plates, cans, and pop bottles.
At the front gate a dejected girl stares at the Closed sign. The
caption had the girl saying, "No fair."

Storm and Shawna laughed so loud that Marbles crawled
under the bed. Gracie and Mick cracked up even though
they'd already seen the cartoon.

Annie didn't get it.

Storm poked Annie's arm. "Come on, Annie! Don't you get
it? 'No fair!' and 'No fair,' as in there's no fair."

"I get that," Annie said. What she didn't get was why they
all thought it was so funny.

When the laughter died down, Gracie announced that she
had to go. "Get going on next week's blog. Annie, don't forget
to rewrite your answer to D.C."

"Your answer was great, Annie," Shawna said. "I hope I didn't — "

"No. You were right, Shawna. Maybe you should help me with the column from now on." Annie was just making conversation, but Gracie's big green eyes got bigger.

"Think about it, Shawna," Gracie said. She turned to Annie. "That school paper your cousin worked on in New Orleans won all kinds of awards. Did you know that?"

Annie hadn't even known Shawna wrote for her school paper. But she wasn't surprised. Nothing Shawna did — or could do — would ever surprise her again.

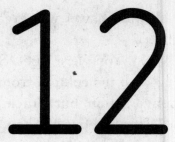

12

A few minutes after the blog team left, the phone rang. Annie let her mom answer. Seconds later Mom shouted, "Phone! It's Storm!"

Annie wondered why Storm hadn't rung her cell. "Be right there!"

"She wants Shawna."

When Annie went to the kitchen to get a drink a half hour later, Shawna was still on the phone. "Storm, think about it. Y'all are like one of those workers who got hired last. You just became a Christian, right? But y'all get the same stuff as Annie and me." Shawna grinned over at Annie. "Your room in heaven will be just as fine as Annie's."

Annie hadn't talked much to Storm about her new faith. She'd been afraid of sounding too pushy. Obviously, that was another fear Shawna didn't share with Annie. She put the juice back in the fridge and walked upstairs to get ready for bed.

The phone rang three more times — all three for Shawna. The last one — the one that came on Annie's cell because the caller didn't bother to look up the house phone number — came from Dallas. Shawna and Dallas were still talking when Annie turned off the light.

The next day Annie worked on heel stretches before breakfast. She was nailing kicks on the ground. How hard would it be in the air?

She and Shawna walked to school in the morning chill. The sun struggled to break through a wet, clingy fog. It might have been almost any month in Ohio, where people said all four seasons could appear on the same day.

At school it was as if Shawna had gone to Big Lake High her whole life. She remembered everyone's name. She'd even done her homework and joined in class discussions.

"Y'all okay, Annie?" Shawna asked as they set down their lunch trays at the cheerleaders' table.

"Fo' sho'!" Annie answered, with more enthusiasm than she felt. She'd always loved game days, when they got to wear their cheerleading uniforms and put on pep rallies. But today she couldn't get into it. When they'd learned their pep rally had been cancelled due to standardized testing, Callie and Amanda had thrown a fit. Annie, on the other hand, discovered she didn't care.

"I can't get over how kickin' y'all's cheerleading outfits are." Shawna glanced around the table. "Y'all must be so excited about the game tonight."

"You're coming, aren't you?" Callie asked, like it really mattered.

"Wouldn't miss it," Shawna assured her. She tried to wave Gracie over to join them.

Gracie shook her head. "Sorry. I don't speak *cheer.*"

Bridget sighed. "Ah. To cheer or not to cheer? What a stupid question."

When the laughter died, they fired questions to Shawna about what it was like to cheer in the South.

"We had to lift weights every day after school," Shawna said. She spread mayonnaise on wheat bread and slapped on ham and swiss. "We only had one weight room, so the football guys were always giving us a hard time, because they could lift more pounds than we could."

"What did you do?" Rakiah asked.

Shawna took a tiny bite of her sandwich and waited until it went down. Everybody at the table leaned in, waiting. "We told them, 'Wimps lift weights. Cheerleaders lift people.'"

This time the girls applauded.

"Enough about me!" Shawna said. "I can't wait to watch you guys cheer tonight. Don't forget. It's not whether you win or lose. It's how you *cheer* the game!"

In history, "Bones," Gracie's blog name for their teacher, Mr. Stovall, tried to get Shawna to talk about Hurricane Katrina. "Would you give the class a feel for what it's like to survive a hurricane?"

Shawna studied her fingernails. It was the first time Annie noticed how short they were. At last, something not perfect about Shawna. "We left the city when they started evacuating."

"Well, tell us about that then," Bones urged. "Weren't cars backed up for miles trying to get out of New Orleans?"

Gracie leaned in and whispered something to Storm.

Storm, sitting next to Shawna, had her legs crossed. The top leg jiggled faster and faster until she spurted out, "Speaking of cars and traffic jams, did you guys know that traffic lights were invented before cars?"

Shawna smiled over at Storm. "Yeah?"

"Fasheezy! But that's nothing. Peter Durand came up with the idea of canned food in 1810. But the can opener wasn't invented until forty-eight years later! So how did they open all those cans? That's what I want to know, Mr. Stovall."

Bones tried to bring the class back to Hurricane Katrina. He pulled down his wall map and pointed out where the hurricane had struck. "At the time of the hurricane the population of New Orleans was about — "

"Mr. Stovall!" Again Storm interrupted him. "Could we take a peek at the world map, please?"

Bones looked skeptical. "This one?" He lifted the U.S. map to show a map of the world.

"That's the ticket!" Storm exclaimed. "See little China there? We all know China is overpopulated. But did you know that if we sat outside and had the entire population of China walk past us in single file, we wouldn't live long enough to see the end of the line?"

"We'll have to start sending people to other planets!" Shawna said. "Dibs on Pluto. It's the only planet discovered by an American."

"Probably why it has a Disney name," Storm suggested. "And I'm with you, Shawna. Once a planet, always a planet. I don't care what those scientists say about poor Pluto getting kicked out of the planet-hood."

"Miss Novelo, I'm going to have to ask that you not speak for the remainder of our class." Bones had only resorted to this tactic one other time. It hadn't worked then either.

"Now here's what I really don't get!" Storm declared. "Why is it that in England the Speaker of the House isn't allowed to speak?"

Bones beamed. "Because the Speaker's job is to preside."

"Wow!" Storm had never appeared more interested in class. "Go on!"

And Bones did. For the rest of the class he explained the ins and outs of parliamentary procedure. Not another word about Hurricane Katrina.

After school the cheerleaders ran through routines while they waited for game time. Annie started to feel like her old self again. She really did love to cheer. She loved the sound of the bleachers filling, the squeak of tennis shoes, the *thump* of the balls as teams warmed up.

During warm-ups some of the cheerleaders ganged up on Shawna and tried to get her to do a full. Bridget had even brought her big sister's old cheerleading uniform for Shawna. Erika had been almost as tiny as Shawna when she'd flown for the Sharks.

But Shawna refused to perform. She laughed off all offers and saved seats for Annie's mom, Storm, and Mick.

The Sharks squad did their welcome cheer for the visitors, and it went off without a hitch. Then they changed gears and focused on getting the Sharks side of the court fired up. Annie thought it was what she did best. She could make boosters out of 3-year-olds or 103-year-olds.

The Sharks were up by eight at the half. The buzzer sounded, and the players ran to the locker room. The cheerleaders stormed the court to the cheers of the crowd. Annie caught a glimpse of her mom and Shawna talking in the bleachers. She wondered if Shawna was already bored with Midwest cheerleading.

The Big Lake band struck up the halftime music, and Annie stepped into line. She poured it on, kicking as high as she could, springing on each step, shouting loud.

One more count, and it would be time for her to pull the Liberty. Even as she stepped into her bases, Annie couldn't help thinking that there wasn't much to this stunt. It was ordinary. Boring. She wondered what Shawna would have done if she'd been flying tonight.

The crowd blurred. They were a steady roar as Annie was lifted on one leg. She started to bend her free leg for the Liberty. Then suddenly, she kicked straight up for a heel stretch.

"Annie?" Bridget cried.

Annie felt her foot whiz by her ear. She grabbed for her ankle, caught it and pulled up, up, up.

But her other leg, the standing leg, felt like jelly.

Stiff, she told herself. *Stay stiff!*

Her knee wobbled. At the same instant, she felt her raised foot slipping out of her grip. She couldn't hold on. Her foot flopped. Annie swayed. She waved her arms as if she could fly. Seconds felt like hours.

Somebody screamed.

Annie felt hands grabbing for her.

But she was falling. Faster and faster. She shut her eyes and felt it coming.

Smack! Thud!

She couldn't breathe.

Couldn't move.

Couldn't think.

Annie sat on the edge of the bed in the curtained-off emergency room cubical. "Can't we go home now?"

Nobody but Annie's mother had been allowed back with her. "The doctor has to look at your X-rays. Does it hurt too much?"

Annie shrugged. Part of her wanted to cry and let Mommy kiss her arm and make it better. The other part didn't want Mom to worry more than she already was. Besides, she had a small audience in the emergency waiting room. Storm and Shawna had ridden in Mom's car. Annie couldn't remember everything that happened after her fall, but she recalled seeing Dallas standing over her, Coach bringing ice, a couple of cheerleaders crying.

The doctor came back. Her English was good, almost too good to be American English. Annie thought she might have been Indian. "The good news is that your arm is not broken. But you have a jolly good sprain of your wrist." She repositioned the ice bag on Annie's arm. Annie winced. It felt like needles sticking into her bone. "Keep that ice on for a couple of hours. All right?"

"Should I keep her home from school, Doctor?" Mom asked.

"I don't think that will be necessary, although she might want to stay out of crowded hallways for a while. We do not want that wrist reinjured."

Annie's head buzzed. They'd given her something for nausea because she'd thought she was going to hurl. Then they gave her something for pain. She wasn't sure what else. "What about cheering?" she asked.

The doctor frowned at her. "Excuse me?"

"I'm okay to cheer, right?"

"Annie!" Her mom started to reach for her, then recoiled as if afraid to touch her. "There's no way I'm letting you — "

"It's just my wrist! And it's not even broken!" Annie's heart pounded. She could almost feel the medicines racing through her veins. She wheeled on the doctor. "It's just a sprain, right?"

"Yes," the doctor began, "but — "

"Well then? I've cheered with a sprained ankle before. Most of us have!"

The doctor glanced up at Annie's mom. "This is true. I have bandaged many cheerleaders who continue to cheer."

"Which just shows how dangerous the whole thing is," Mom concluded.

"It's not dangerous!" Annie knew she was shouting, but she couldn't help herself. "I *have* to cheer in competition, Mom!" Tears came, and she tried to sniff them back.

Her mom dropped her head and took a deep breath. Annie knew she was praying. "Doctor, why don't you tell us if it's safe for Annie to go back to cheerleading or not."

Annie started to object, but her mother's glare stopped her.

The doctor touched the bandage she'd wrapped from Annie's wrist to her elbow. On top of that, Annie had another bandage that looked like a big, stiff glove with the fingers cut out. "I want you to keep the arm bandaged for forty-eight hours. And you must wear the wrist brace until I see you again."

"So I'm okay to cheer?" Annie swiped at her tears with the back of her good hand.

The doctor shook her head. "You do those cartwheels and flips, yes?"

"Not in competition. I'm the flyer. Other girls lift me up."

"Which means she could fall again," Mom added.

"I won't!" Annie promised.

Again her mom looked down and breathed deeply.

"Nothing for forty-eight hours. Absolute," the doctor ordered.

Annie figured fast in her head. That meant no practice tomorrow or Thursday. But if she could make Friday's practice, she could still compete on Saturday. "So if I take off two days, I can still do competition?"

"With your wrist brace on."

Annie's mom obviously didn't like this answer. "But what if she falls again?"

"It is a risk," the doctor admitted. "But the wrist isn't broken. In the end, it is your decision."

They made an appointment to see the doctor in her office the following week. Then they walked out to the waiting room, where Annie was mobbed by the whole blog team, plus Dallas and Shawna and Ms. Whitney.

Wednesday it took Annie forever to get dressed. Her wrist throbbed. Every time she forgot and reached for something, a

stabbing pain shot up her arm. Mom drove the girls to school.
The sky fell in layers of pink, white, and blue. A strong west
wind blew in spring and the scent of grass pushing at the earth.

"I can get someone to watch the shop for me so I can pick
you up after school," Mom suggested.

"That's okay, Mom. Thanks. But I can walk home after
cheerleading practice."

"After *what?*" The car swerved, but Mom got it back.

"I'm just going to watch. I promise."

"I'll tag along just to make sure," Shawna offered.

Mom did the breathing-praying thing again. "Okay. I'll see
you at dinner then."

As soon as they got out of the car, Shawna fell into step
with Annie. "I didn't ask last night. Y'all were kind of out of
it. Annie, how did it happen?"

Annie didn't answer.

"I mean, the fall. Y'all were doing so great. Then ... it was
like you lost your balance. Was it your bases? Did Bridget
come in late? Because I saw her do it in practice once and — "

"I tried a heel stretch." Even saying the words made Annie
quiver inside. Her brain flashed her photos of those last
seconds as she grabbed at the air to stay up. She shook her
head to get rid of the pictures.

"But why? Y'all hadn't practiced it in the mount. Why
would you try it at a game?"

"I didn't plan it, Shawna."

They didn't say anything else. Annie didn't want to talk
to Shawna about cheerleading. She didn't want to talk to
Shawna about anything.

After last class Annie headed for the gym. Her arm ached from holding her wrist funny. And the skin under the bandage itched. Her good arm didn't feel that great either, since it had done the work of two arms all day. Still, Annie needed to go to practice. She couldn't "get back on the horse." Not yet. But the longer she stayed away, the more scared she'd get.

"Hold up, Annie!" Shawna caught her outside the gym. "Why didn't y'all wait for me?"

"Sorry. I didn't know you'd want to go to practice again."

Storm came strolling up. "Hey, I don't know why either of you would ever cheer. Period."

"Don't start," Shawna warned.

"Storm," Annie pleaded, "it was just a fall."

"I'm just saying," Storm continued. "Twenty thousand injuries last year. Fifty-two percent were strains or sprains, but three percent were concussions. And sixteen percent fractures. Don't forget you're more likely to get hurt in a cheerleading toss than you are in a football tackle."

Annie tried to let Storm's stats roll off her. Storm was statistic crazy. "So what, Storm? You think I should quit cheering?"

"Only if you want to live to be a junior." Storm threw her hands in the air. "Don't say I didn't warn you."

Annie watched her walk away, her long braid swishing, the bells on her boots jingling.

"I'm going in," Annie said.

"And I promised Aunt Sam I'd keep an eye on y'all. Besides, I like watching practice." Shawna held the door open for her.

"Thanks," Annie muttered. But she didn't need anybody holding the door for her. She wasn't a cripple. One more day off and she'd be back at practice.

Ms. Whitney dropped the mat she'd been dragging onto the floor and came over to Annie. "I didn't expect to see you here. How's the arm?"

"Not bad, thanks. The doctor said I can practice on Friday and still make the competition Saturday. I'm fine as long as I dance or fly. No flips or cartwheels."

"You don't do much with those anyway," Bridget added. She stared at Annie's brace. "You sure it's okay for you to come back?"

Annie's hands clenched automatically, sending a shooting pain through her wrist. It took all she had not to cry out. "I'm sure. But thanks so much for the concern, Bridget."

Bridget shrugged and walked away.

Annie and Shawna looked on as the girls ran through the dance routine. In her head, Annie did the counts, her toes moving with the steps. She didn't want to forget anything. During the tumbling she cheered for each performance.

But when they got to the spot in the routine where the bases gathered for the Elevator, Annie could barely watch. She pictured herself being popped into the air, then floundering, thrashing, and falling.

"Ms. Whitney!" Bridget complained. "This isn't working! I feel like an idiot being a base without a flyer!"

Annie had to admit that they did look pretty out of line dipping and popping with nobody going up.

Ms. Whitney stopped the routine, tugged on one ear, and stared at the bases. "I know what you're saying. But I can't let any of you stand in for Annie. You need to practice your own positions."

Bridget glanced over at the bleachers. "What about Shawna?"

Annie felt something warm rise in her stomach. She swallowed hard.

"That's a great idea!" Amanda agreed.

The others murmured their approval.

"Shawna!" Callie shouted. "How 'bout it? Wanna fly?"

"Annie's good to go on Friday!" Shawna shouted back.

Ms. Whitney started walking toward them. "You know, it might help if you stood in. Just until Annie's back."

Shawna turned to Annie. Her eyes shone. "What do you think, Annie?"

"Do what you want to, Shawna. Don't ask me."

"I won't do it if you don't want me to."

"I don't care." As the words came out, flat and unemotional, Annie wondered if she'd ever told a bigger lie.

Shawna sprang to her feet. "I'll do it!"

Her fans cheered.

"Just until Friday," Shawna added, smiling back at Annie.

Annie couldn't watch. There was no way she could stay and see Shawna rise in the Elevator, *her* Elevator, doing fantastic stunts to the cheers of the Sharks cheerleaders. She stood up and headed for the door, half-expecting Shawna or Rakiah or somebody to try to stop her.

Nobody did.

Annie rushed outside. Her chest burned. Her eyes blurred with tears. Her arm felt like a dead tree trunk, too heavy to lift.

Shawna. If Shawna hadn't tried to get her to do a heel stretch, none of this would have happened. If Shawna hadn't shown off all her stunts, Annie wouldn't have tried something new at the game. She wouldn't have fallen. She wouldn't have been walking out right now.

Annie knew in her head it wasn't true. Yet everything — from the throbbing in her arm to the pain and ache in her heart — felt like Shawna's fault.

14

By Thursday Annie's wrist was already feeling better. She sat at the kitchen table before school while Mom rewrapped the Ace bandage. "What about this stupid wrist brace?" Annie asked. She wiggled her fingers. "See? That doesn't even hurt anymore."

"The brace stays, Annie," Mom said. "But I'm glad you're feeling better."

"I'm feeling fine. There's no reason I can't cheer today." Shawna hadn't said a word about her time flying, and Annie hadn't asked. All she wanted was to get back to it. She'd had a dream, more like a nightmare, about her fall. If she didn't get back up and fly soon, she'd be afraid to do it. Forever.

"Annie, we've been all over this. We're going to do what the doctor ordered. If we did what *I* want, you'd stay out all year. At least."

Annie knew Mom wasn't kidding. "I know. Thanks for not going there."

Mom hugged her, and it felt good.

"Hey! Can I get in on that?" Shawna wormed her way into their hug.

Annie backed off. "I better get ready."

At school it wasn't hard for Annie to keep her distance from Shawna. She doubted her cousin even noticed. Liam trailed after Shawna. If she wasn't talking to him, she was hanging with one of the cheerleaders.

After school Annie didn't know whether to torture herself and watch cheerleading practice or not. She stayed in the library while the halls cleared. Rain pelted the roof. It sounded like tin cans dragging behind a pickup. Annie didn't particularly feel like walking home in a downpour.

There was no sign of Shawna when Annie came out of the library.

"What are *you* doing here?"

Annie wheeled around to see Storm, loaded down with books. "I can read too, you know," Annie snapped.

"I just meant I thought you'd be at your daredevil practice," Storm countered. She knelt and loaded her books into plastic bags.

"I'm heading down there. I guess."

"I may stop by too. I hear Shawna's going to get down and fancy. Throw some New Orleans cheerleading jazz at the Sharks. Not that I approve," she added quickly. "I just need a place to hang until this rain lets up."

They walked together to the gym. Halfway there Annie heard the cheers: "Go, Shawna!" "That's so fly!"

"Guess they started without us, huh?" Storm said.

Then, as if someone had turned off the sound, the gym went silent. Annie and Storm walked in, their footsteps echoing. The girls were crowded into a semicircle, their backs to Annie so she couldn't see what they were looking at. Then Shawna rose from the center, high above their heads, extended by the bases. She kicked her leg high, and Annie thought she was doing a heel stretch. Instead, she reached

over her head with one arm and held the opposite foot in a
perfect standing splits. When she stuck out her other arm,
her body formed a Bow and Arrow. To Annie, it seemed like
Shawna stayed suspended in the Bow and Arrow for minutes
before dropping into a basket dismount.

But she wasn't done yet. Shawna righted herself for the
Elevator lift. This time she did an Arabesque. Then she rose
again and pulled a Scorpion, kicking her free leg behind her
so high that she grabbed her foot with both hands above her
head, forming a Scorpion's Tail. Ms. Whitney had said it was
the hardest stunt ever.

"That's got to hurt," Storm commented. She said something
else, but it got lost in the hoots and howls that broke out from
the cheerleaders.

"I need to go home," Annie told Storm.

"What?" Storm shouted.

Annie smiled and waved, then got out of there as fast as she
could.

Outside, rain struck sideways. Annie didn't even try to
stay dry. Her big feet slapped through puddles and sloshed
through mud. Thunder rumbled, shaking her bones as she cut
through the field for home.

Why did you bring her here, God? The words rumbled like
thunder in her heart. *I wanted a sister. I couldn't wait for Shawna
to come to Big Lake! I just didn't know she'd be ... she'd be so much
better at everything than I am. You made both of us. Why did she get
the little feet? Why am I so clumsy? I could never do what she does
cheering!*

She kicked at a puddle. Water shot straight up, splashing
her to the neck. *Just great. Here I am with a sprained wrist and*

*no talent and feet the size of North and South Carolina. And she's
back there flying in my place! Is that fair? I don't want her here, God!
Send her back to her own home. Her own cheerleading squad. Her own
friends. Her own dog. Even Marbles likes her best!*

The air had drained from Annie's anger balloon by the
time she opened the door to her house. Marbles lunged at her,
nearly knocking her over.

Annie sat on the floor and buried her face in the shaggy
dog's warm neck. Now that the flames of anger were
smoldering, she could think a little more clearly. "Marbles,"
she said, scratching the dog behind his ear until his back
leg thumped with pleasure, "I just griped to God that you
like Shawna best. How's that for being a good human?" She
cringed thinking about the other things she'd yelled at God.
Sorry about that, Father, she prayed.

A kind of calm settled over her. She listened to the noises
of her house. The *thump, thumping* of Marbles' foot on the
hardwood floor. The ticking of the grandfather clock. The
cranky noise the pipes made for no reason. All safe, warm
sounds, while the storm threw frustrated rain showers at the
house fortress.

Annie kissed Marbles' head. "We're pretty lucky we've got
a God who lets us say whatever we're feeling. You know that,
Marbles?" She got to her feet. "How about I get out of these
wet clothes and get us both something to eat?"

Marbles followed Annie to her room then out to the
kitchen, where Annie made them ham sandwiches. She was
on her second glass of milk when she heard the front door.
"Mom?"

But it wasn't Mom. Shawna and Storm burst in.

Storm's long hair was plastered to her head. "I told Shawna we could call somebody to give us a ride. But she didn't want to wait."

Shawna didn't say anything. She just stood inside the door and shivered, water dripping from her.

"I'll get you something to dry off with," Annie said. She grabbed beach towels from the linen closet and went back to the living room. "There." She tossed both towels.

Storm caught one, and the other fell at Shawna's feet. When Shawna made no move to pick it up, Storm did it for her and wrapped the towel around her shoulders. "It's wicked out there," Storm observed. "Impressive storm."

Annie couldn't help but notice that even soaking wet, her cousin would have looked good on the cover of a teen magazine.

Shawna frowned at the towel like she couldn't remember how it got around her shoulders. "Thanks," she muttered.

"I didn't think you'd be done already," Annie said. By her calculations, practice should have been ending right about now.

"Where did you go?" Shawna asked. "I hardly saw you all day. I thought you were going to watch practice."

"You didn't need me," Annie mumbled.

Storm bent in half and rubbed her long hair in the towel.

"What?" Shawna asked.

Annie raised her voice. "I said you didn't need me. You had enough fans to watch your show."

Storm cleared her throat. "Okay! Why don't we all go get something to eat?" She wrapped her hair into the towel in a makeshift turban.

"Annie?" Shawna demanded. "What's the matter with you? You've been acting like you're mad at me all day."

Annie didn't deny it, and she didn't look away.

"What did I do?" Shawna whined.

"What did you do? Do you mean besides a Bow and Arrow and a Scorpion? I can't answer that because I ducked out before the show was over."

"You saw that?"

"Yeah. If I hadn't, I would have heard about it. Congratulations, Shawna. You're the talk of the town. Everybody in Big Lake loves you."

As if to prove her point, Marbles turned in circles then lunged at Shawna and licked her face.

"Told you!" Annie glanced up at the ceiling. "See?" Her heart pounded. Her ears roared. She couldn't hear herself think.

"Annie, what are you talking about?" Shawna cried.

"Seriously, Annie," Storm agreed. "Ease off."

"I might have known you'd take Shawna's side!" Annie accused. She felt walled off from the whole world, from her friends, from everything. Storm and Shawna had become best friends in less than a week. "I just can't believe this whole thing happened so fast!"

"What happened so fast?" Storm asked.

"Everything was fine," Annie said. "Last week I was so happy ..."

"Last week?" Shawna repeated.

"Now I've lost my friends, my dog, and my cheerleading spot," Annie concluded. "It's not fair."

Storm grinned. "Now where have I heard those words before?"

Annie was in no mood for Storm's humor.

Suddenly, Marbles stopped licking Shawna and cowered on the floor. He covered his head with his big paws. A second later a siren went off. Loud. Wailing. It was the same siren that sounded every Saturday at noon for emergency alert testing.

"What is it?" Shawna screamed.

"You think it's a test?" Storm asked.

Annie walked to the window and stared out at a changed world. Nothing moved. Limbs and leaves that had swayed with the wind and rain now stood still. The gray had turned to a sickly yellow, tinting trees, grass, sidewalk, everything. The yellow cast washed over the sky, where black clouds raced and grew more fierce, puffed up with their own power.

The phone rang. "I'll get it." Annie jogged to the kitchen. "Hello?"

"Annie?" The phone crackled. Mom's voice sounded scared.

"Yeah?"

"Are you okay? Are you by yourself?"

"Shawna and Storm are here."

"Good. You need to get to the basement. *Now!*"

"The basement? Why?"

"Annie! Don't argue! Can't you hear the sirens? It's a tornado!"

15

Annie returned to the living room. The rotating siren wailed loud, then softer, then louder again. "We need to get to the basement."

"Why?" Shawna shouted.

"It's not a test. It's a tornado warning," Annie explained.

"A tornado?" Shawna cried.

"Don't freak, Shawna," Storm said. "I haven't been in Ohio that long, and I've already been in three of these warnings."

Annie led the way through the kitchen to the basement stairs. The only reason anyone ever went into the gross basement was for laundry. Grandpa Lind planned to finish the basement one of these days. The damp, concrete floor and green-gray walls smelled like rotten potatoes.

Annie pulled the string on the lightbulb that hung over the stairs. Empty suitcases and over-filled boxes sat in one corner, with the washer and dryer in the other. She grabbed towels out of the laundry basket and dropped them on the floor. "We should sit in this corner."

"Pretty creepy," Storm observed. "How long do you think it will last?" She plopped onto one of the towels. "Shawna?"

Annie spotted Shawna standing in shadows on the stairs. "You shouldn't stay there."

Shawna didn't move. She had her arms wrapped around herself as if to keep from shattering.

Annie wanted to stay angry. Shawna had taken everything from her. Maybe not on purpose. But it hurt just the same. Yet she looked so helpless. "Shawna, come and sit with us."

The light went out. Shawna screamed.

Annie felt her way over to the stairs. "It's okay. I'm coming. Don't worry. It's just the electricity. Shawna? Where are you? I can't see." Her hands felt through the black. She rammed into something with her shin. Then her bad wrist hit the banister.

She felt Shawna's arm and took it. "Come down two steps. Stay close." Annie had to pull gently on her arm, but Shawna took a step down. Then another. And she was off the stairs.

Annie tried to aim toward the corner. "Storm? Where are you?"

"Over here! In the dark. I'll whistle you over." Storm whistled a song Annie didn't recognize, but it served the purpose.

"Made it." Annie put her hands on Shawna's shoulders and guided her to the towel next to Storm.

"You okay?" Storm asked. "Gracie told me tornadoes always miss Big Lake. All we get are warnings."

"You don't know that!" Shawna snapped. "You get warning after warning. And you think nothing will ever happen. A warning is just a warning. And then one day one of those warnings is for real. And it really happens!"

Annie had never seen Shawna like this. "Shawna? What are you talking about?" But she thought she knew. Her cousin had more on her mind than just the tornado.

"We heard them too." Shawna's voice grew softer, but turned flat. "The sirens."

"Go on," Annie urged. The whole time Shawna had been in Ohio, she'd never talked about the hurricane. Annie hadn't asked. Maybe she should have.

"My dad started flipping channels to local stations. I remember that I'd been watching that chocolate factory movie, and I didn't want him to change channels. Isn't that silly? I was mad at him because he interrupted my movie. Everybody gave different reports. Some said we should get out of New Orleans fast. Others said we should stay home and off the highways."

Annie scooted closer to Shawna and felt her shivering. She put one arm around her and touched Storm's arm in the clammy darkness of the basement.

"At first we thought we'd wait it out. Dad boarded the windows. We'd done it before. It was never as bad as they said it was going to be." Outside the siren moaned. Above them, the basement ceiling creaked. "So we waited," Shawna said. "And watched. It rained harder and harder."

Annie's eyes were getting used to the dark. She could see the outline of Shawna's face as it turned toward her.

"That rain. It was all I could think about today. Every time I saw the rain or heard it at school, I thought I'd go crazy. I thought it would never stop. The only time I didn't think about the rain was when I was in the air. Flying."

Annie understood. There was nothing like it, when her head cleared and then filled with joy so there wasn't room for anything else.

"I can't remember it all," Shawna continued. "We waited until they ordered everybody to evacuate. Some people had no way to get out. Dad crammed neighbors and strangers into our car until not another person fit. I was crying. I yelled that I didn't want to leave because we couldn't take Mitzi, our black lab. They had to carry me to the car. There was barely room for me."

"What happened to your dog?" Storm asked.

Shawna's words got stuck in her throat. When they came out, the words sounded squeezed together. "I ... I don't know. We called and wrote letters. The Humane Society has Mitzi's description and our e-mail."

Annie couldn't imagine losing Marbles that way. And here she'd been jealous of Marbles' attention to Shawna.

"Then what?" Storm asked.

"Mr. Stovall was right. Y'all wouldn't believe the back up on every road leading out of New Orleans. We sat packed into that car for hours. It was so hot."

The siren seemed to grow louder. Shawna covered her ears. Her whole body trembled.

"I think we should pray," Annie said. She had no idea what to pray or what to say next. But she knew they all needed to talk to God and to listen to him. *Father, please protect us. Help Shawna know you're right here with us. We don't know your will, but we know you. And you're bigger than any tornado.*

There was more she needed to say. *I'm so sorry for the way I've been acting. Please forgive me for being jealous of Shawna.* Annie remembered crying out to God about the way the cheerleaders, her friends, and even her dog liked Shawna best. And all the while, Shawna had lost *her* friends, her dog, her home and school. *"I can't believe I —"*

"Father, I need to ask you to forgive me," Shawna interrupted. *"I've been so envious of Annie."*

Annie opened her eyes and stared at Shawna, who sat hunched over, like she was waiting for the plane to crash.

"God," Shawna continued, *"I love my parents. But Aunt Sam is something different. She gets us. I can talk to her. And Granny and*

Gramps. And this home. I was jealous that Annie has lived here her whole life. She has the best friends, who love her and think the world of her."

Annie couldn't believe it. Shawna had been envying *her*?

"I've been such a coward." Shawna talked to God as if he were the only one in the basement with her. Annie didn't want to interrupt. *"Every time it's rained, all I can think about is that hurricane. But Annie? She's not afraid of anything."*

"Okay. That does it!" Annie said.

Storm and Shawna looked up. Their faces glowed in light that now streamed through the smudged, lone window high on the nearest wall.

"How could you think I'm not afraid of anything?" Annie asked. "I've been scared to death since the day you arrived in Big Lake."

"Scared of what?" Shawna asked.

"Of how perfect you are, for one thing!" Annie answered. "And scared of flying, for another."

"Huh-uh," Shawna replied.

"I fell in practice the day you got here. It took everything I had to get in the mount again. Then I fell again!"

"Annie, you should have said."

"I did."

Shawna frowned, then shook her head. "You did, didn't you? You asked me that question about being afraid. I guess I wasn't listening. I'm sorry, Annie."

"Me too. I wasn't listening either," Annie admitted. She pulled Shawna into a hug. "I was too busy envying you."

"Whoa!" Storm bounced up and twirled around. "You guys! Can you believe this? It's exactly like that verse! It's almost spooky, don't you think? Man!"

"What verse?" Shawna asked.

"The one Mick posted on *That's What You Think!* About envying each other and being jealous. And thinking *No fair!* Man, this Bible stuff really rocks!"

Annie laughed. "True dat!" She turned to Shawna. "When I saw you doing that Scorpion, I would have given anything to be you."

"You're kidding?" Shawna leaned back and gazed at Annie. "What a waste that would be! There's only one Annie Lind, and she's amazing." She sat cross-legged, the stiffness in her limbs gone now. "Dad said once that if we try to be someone else, we can't ever be us, the people God wants us to be."

"Makes sense," Annie admitted. "Your dad must be pretty smart."

Shawna smiled. "I miss my dad. And my mom. So much! I love it here. And you guys have been great. But I hate being separated from my parents."

"Hey! Shush!" Storm put her finger to her lips. "Hear that?"

Annie listened. "I don't hear anything."

"Exactly!" Storm exclaimed.

Shawna got to her feet. "The siren stopped! So did the rain! Does that mean it's over?"

Marbles barked. Annie heard the front door. Footsteps passed overhead. The basement door opened, and Annie's mom hollered down, "Girls! Annie? Are you down there? We got the all clear!"

They ran up the steps just as the lights came back on.

Annie's mom shut the basement door behind them. "Everybody okay? I was so scared."

Shawna winked at Annie. "We know just how you felt, Aunt Sam."

"You're soaking wet," Mom cried. "Go change. You too, Storm. Annie can find something for you to wear."

"But will it be as fashionable as paisley pants and my flowered shirt?" Storm asked.

"Go!" Mom ordered. "I've got something I need to talk to Shawna about."

They changed and joined Mom at the kitchen table, where mugs of hot chocolate waited.

"This must be serious if you've brought out the mini-marshmallows," Annie observed.

"I have some news," her mom began. "Good news for Shawna, not so good for us. Shawna, I've been talking to your parents. We didn't want to say anything to you until it was all settled."

"Is something wrong?" Shawna asked.

"No. Everything's fine. Except they miss you like crazy, honey."

"I miss them too." Her eyes clouded with tears.

Annie reached over and put her bandaged hand on top of Shawna's.

"Well, a couple of things have happened," Mom continued. "Looks like people are starting to rebuild your dad's church."

"That's great!" Shawna exclaimed.

"And your parents wound up their work in France. Honey, they want to come back here, pick you up, and move back to New Orleans."

16

"When are Shawna's parents coming for her?" Annie asked.

"Monday," Mom answered. "They'll stay a few days and visit. But they want to move back as soon as they can."

It was happening too fast. Annie couldn't get a handle on it.

"What about her school?" Storm asked. "Are they rebuilding that too?"

Mom shook her head. "I don't think so. Not yet." She turned to Shawna. "Your parents want to homeschool you next year while things are getting back to normal."

"Cool!" Storm exclaimed. "I had a friend where we lived before. Her mom homeschooled her, and she only studied a couple hours a day."

Annie didn't like the sound of this. "What about school activities? Like cheering?"

"It will be okay, Annie." Shawna turned to Sam. "Are they really coming Monday?"

Annie's mom nodded.

Shawna smiled at Annie. "At least I'll get to see you in competition Saturday. I'm going to miss you, cousin."

Annie couldn't keep back the tears. She'd finally gotten the sister she'd always wanted. And now she was moving away. "I can't believe you're leaving."

"I'll come back," Shawna promised.

"You better!" Storm said.

"And y'all can come visit me in New Orleans!"

"Will we have to talk like that if we come?" Storm teased.

That night after Storm left, Annie and Shawna ran through the Sharks' competition dance routine for Annie's mom. Then they worked on heel stretches. Not for the competition. But someday Annie knew she'd get there.

With lights out, Annie stared at the moon shadows on the ceiling. "Shawna? You asleep?"

"Huh-uh."

"What if I freeze up there tomorrow at practice? Or get scared again?"

"You won't. Just remember, you won't be up there alone."

The thought, the promise, floated around Annie's room and danced in the moon shadows.

At Friday's practice Annie braced herself. She figured nobody would be glad to have her back on the team after they'd had Shawna. But she was wrong. They cheered when she walked in. Only Bridget asked if she was *sure* she was ready to perform.

Shawna looked on as the Sharks ran through the dance routine and the tumbles.

When they got to the end of the routine, right before she stepped into the Elevator, Annie smiled at Shawna. Then she felt the dip, the pop. And she was flying. She did the toe touch, her favorite stunt. Down she went again. Then up, pulling poses and making faces. For the finale, as the bases extended her, she kept her body straight, tucked one knee, and raised her arms in the Liberty. Her heart filled with thanksgiving for the joy she felt. She was where she wanted to be, *who* she wanted to be.

When it was all over and even Bridget had congratulated her, Annie still felt the glow of flying. She couldn't imagine Shawna not having that again. Annie wasn't sure what was fair and what wasn't anymore. Sometimes things just were.

But not always. Sometimes there was something you could do.

"Ms. Whitney?" Annie waved her coach to the sidelines.

"What is it, Annie?" Ms. Whitney looked worried. "Are you okay?"

"I'm fine. But I was wondering if we could let Shawna compete in my place tomorrow?"

"Why? Is something wrong?"

"Everything's right," Annie answered. "It's just that I'll have the rest of the year to compete. Shawna won't. She's going back to New Orleans, but her school's gone. This may be her last chance to fly. Please?"

"I don't know, Annie. There are rules of competition. She'd have to stick to our routine. Nothing fancy. Toe touch. The Lib. I can make some calls."

"Tell them about Shawna and the hurricane."

Ms. Whitney nodded slowly. Then she smiled. "I think the country's made some exceptions for the hurricane victims. We all feel for them. Let me see what I can do."

"That was a nice thing you did," Annie mom's said as they waited for the competition to begin on Saturday. They were sitting with the whole blog team for the Ohio Cheer Explosion. The auditorium was filled with people cheering the cheerleaders from area schools.

"I thought you were up to something," Storm said. "You couldn't wait to get back to your daredevil cheering. Then all of a sudden your arm isn't quite up to it?"

"Hey. I never told Shawna my wrist was too bad to cheer. I just said she needed to take over for me. Shawna drew her own conclusions. Besides, if I hadn't let her think I wasn't good to go, she never would have taken my place."

"Not bad, Annie," Gracie said.

Mick passed around sticks of gum. "I think it's great."

"Enough already," Jazz said. "Sharks are up."

The Sharks rocked. Annie couldn't help imagining what it would have felt like to rise in the Elevator, with all eyes on the flyer. Part of her yearned to jump off the bleachers and take back her spot.

But there was something else going on inside her. Something new. As she watched the joy on Shawna's face, high in a perfect Liberty, Annie felt it too. It was an amazing discovery. When envy was gone — snuffed out — something else replaced it. Joy. She was sharing Shawna's joy. God was so generous. There was plenty of joy to go around.

Internet Safety by Michaela

People aren't always what they seem at first, like wolves in sheep's clothing. Chat rooms, blogs, and other places online can be fun ways to meet all kinds of people with all kinds of interests. But be aware and cautious. Here are some tips to help keep you safe while surfing the web, keeping a blog, chatting online, and writing e-mails.

- Never give out personal information such as your address, phone number, parents' work addresses or phone numbers, or the name and address of your school without your parents' or guardian's permission. It's okay to talk about your likes and dislikes, but keep private information just that—private.

- Before you agree to meet someone in person, first check with your parents or guardian to make sure it's okay. A safe way to meet for the first time is to bring a parent or guardian with you.

- You might be tempted to send a picture of yourself to new friends you've met online. Just in case your acquaintance is not who you think they are, check with your parent or guardian before you hit send.

- If you feel uncomfortable by angry, threatening, or other types of e-mails or posts addressed to you, tell your parent or guardian immediately.

- Before you promise to call a new friend on the telephone, talk to your parent or guardian first.

- Remember that just because you might read about something or someone online doesn't mean the information is true. Sometimes people say cruel or untruthful things just to be mean.

- If someone writes creepy posts, report him or her to the blog or website owner.

Following these tips will help keep you safe while you hang out online. If you're careful, you can learn a lot and meet tons of new people.

Subject: Michaela Jenkins

Age: 13 on May 19, 7th grade at Big Lake Middle School
Hair/Eyes: Dark brown hair/Brown eyes
Height: 5'

"Mick the Munch" is content and rooted in her relationship with Christ. She lives with her stepsis, Grace Doe, in the blended family of Gracie's dad and Mick's mom. She's a tomboy, an avid Cleveland Indians fan, and the only girl on her school's baseball team. A computer whiz, Mick keeps *That's What You Think!* up and running. She also helps out at Sam's Sammich Shop and manages to show her friends what deep faith looks like.

Subject: Grace Doe

Age: 15 on August 19, sophomore
Hair/Eyes: Blonde hair/Hazel eyes
Height: 5' 5"

Grace doesn't think she is cute at all. The word "average" was meant for her. She dresses in neutral colors and camouflage to blend in. Grace does not wear makeup. She prefers to observe life rather than participate in it. A bagger at a grocery store, only her close friends and family can get away with calling her "Gracie." She is part of a blended family and lives with her dad and stepmom, two stepsiblings, and two half brothers. Her mother's job frequently keeps her out of town.

Subject: Annie Lind

Age: 16 on October 1, sophomore
Hair/Eyes: Auburn hair/Blue eyes
Height: 5' 10"

Annie desperately wants guys to admire and like her. She is boy-crazy and thinks she always has to be in love. She considers herself to be an expert in matters of the heart. Annie takes being popular for granted because she has always been well-liked. She loves and admires her mom. Her dad was killed in a plane crash when Annie was two months old. Annie helps out at Sam's Sammich Shop, her mom's restaurant. She can be self-centered, though without being selfish.

Subject: Jasmine Fletcher

Age: 15 on July 13, freshman
Hair/Eyes: Black hair/Brown eyes
Height: 5' 6"

Jasmine is an artist who feels that no one, especially her art teacher and parents, understands her art. She is African American, and has great fashion sense, without being trendy. Her parents are quite well-to-do, and they won't let Jasmine get a job. She has a younger brother and a sister who has Down syndrome. She also had a brother who was killed in a drive-by shooting in the old neighborhood when Jazz was one.

Subject: Storm Novello

Age: 14 on September 1, freshman
Hair/Eyes: Brown hair/Dark brown eyes
Height: 5' 2"

Storm doesn't realize how pretty she is. She wishes she had blonde hair. She is Mayan/Mestisa, and claims to be a Mayan princess. Storm always needs to be the center of attention and doesn't let on how smart she is. She dresses in bright, flouncy clothing, and wears too much makeup. Storm is a completely different person around her parents. She changes into her clothes and puts her makeup on after leaving for school. Her parents are very loving, though they have little money.

Here's a sneak preview of the next book
in the Faithgirlz! Blog On series.

1

Jasmine Fletcher dipped her brush into the color she'd invented, "grownck" — a mixture of gray, brown, and black — and applied the final touch to her latest masterpiece. It had taken her all month, but she'd finally created a textured abstract that captured the smell of the school cafeteria. She called it *Hot Lunch*.

All she had left to do was sign her painting. She traded to a fine-point brush, chose grownck, and painted the letters: "J-A-Z — "

"Jasmine?" The knock and door opening struck at the exact same moment, the moment of her signing *Jazz*. The last *Z* jerked and slid like a lightning bolt down the side of her painting.

"It's ruined!" she cried, frantically reaching for a paint rag. She felt, rather than saw, the presence of her mother behind her.

"Jasmine, I'm not your answering service."

"How could you be? You don't wait for answers. You just barge on in," Jazz muttered, dabbing at the stray streak of paint. She'd caught it before it dried, so the damage wasn't too bad. She could fix it.

"What did you say, Jasmine? Don't mumble."

Jazz didn't feel like getting into it with her mother. They'd been at each other more than usual lately, and the whole week of Easter break stretched in front of them. She wiped off the last bit of paint, wadded her rag, and turned to face her mother.

Tosha Fletcher was synonymous with style and sophistication. She wore a tailored pinstripe skirt and jacket, and her hair curved magically into a knot at the base of her neck. Jazz's hair waved and curled at all angles, and that was the way she liked it. Her mother, of course, hated it.

"Did you want something?" Jazz asked, trying to control her voice.

"I want you to take care of your own business and let me conduct mine."

"That's what I was doing...until I was so rudely interrupted." Jazz knew as soon as the words were out of her mouth that they were fighting words. But she couldn't take them back now, even if she wanted to.

"Interrupted?" Mom's dark eyes narrowed. The skin around her jaw tightened. "Let me tell you about *interrupted*. That's the fourth call from that man. Foley? Or whatever his name is."

"Farley." If she'd really talked to him four times, she should have gotten his name straight, Jazz thought. For once, she kept her thoughts to herself.

"I have work to do, Jasmine. I can't spend the entire weekend fielding phone calls for my daughter. I've left messages all over the house for you to call him back. Why haven't you?"

Jazz had seen the notes. She just hadn't gotten the nerve to call him back. A month earlier she'd practically twisted his arm to get him to hang one of her paintings in his gallery.

"Gallery" wasn't exactly the right word for Mr. Farley's shop. He sold frames and craft kits and how-to booklets, along with a few prints.

"Well? Why haven't you called him back? Apparently, he's going to keep calling until you do. What does he want?"

"You're the one who talked to him. Didn't he tell you?" But Jazz felt pretty sure she knew why he was calling. That was why she kept putting off calling him back. When Mr. Farley had agreed to hang her painting in his store, he'd given the experiment one month. The month was up. It was time for her to take back her painting. She'd really had high hopes of selling it too.

"Jasmine, don't take that tone with me." Her mother took in a deep breath.

Jazz started to defend herself. Then instead, she turned her back on her mother and stuck her brushes in the cleaning jar. "Mr. Farley just wants me to pick up my painting."

"Then go pick it up."

Jazz sloshed her brushes in the turpentine and watched the clear liquid take on the tint of grownck.

"Now, Jasmine! Before that man calls here again."

Jazz sighed. "All right." She might as well get it over with. Besides, any creative juices had dried up under the piercing glare of her mother.

Just Jazz

Softcover • ISBN 0-310-71095-2

Jazz is working on a masterpiece: herself... Jasmine "Jazz" Fletcher is an artist down to her toes; she sees beauty and art where others see nothing. And her work on the website is drawing rave reviews. But if she doesn't come up with a commercially successful masterpiece pretty soon, her parents may make her drop what they consider an expensive hobby to focus on a real job.

Storm Rising

Softcover • ISBN 0-310-71096-0

Nobody knows the real Storm... not even Storm! The center of attention wherever she goes, Storm Novelo is impetuous, daring, loud—and a phony. Convinced that no one would like her inner brainiac, she hides her genius behind her public airhead.

Grace Under Pressure

Softcover • ISBN 0-310-71263-7

Gracie's always been good at handling everything herself, but pressures at school and personal disappointments prove almost more than she can bear in this fifth book in the Blog On series. Will she learn to share her burdens with God and with her friends before she cracks?

able now at your local bookstore!

zonderkidz

faiThGirLz!
2 corinthians 4:18

Inner Beauty, Outward Faith

Visit **faithgirlz.com**—
it's the place for girls ages 8-12!

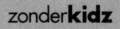